HEIRESS OF THE MAGICAL
FAIRSHAW LIBRARY

HEIRESS

of the

MAGICAL FAIRSHAW LIBRARY

A COZY MAGICAL HISTORICAL FANTASY ROMANCE

AUSTIN RYAN

Publisher: Willowmere Books
Cover design: Willowmere Books
Interior design: Wyvern Wing Press
Editing: Savanna Roberts/SnowRidge Press

Paperback ISBN: 979-8-9852842-4-9

For Besten, Per
Skjæveland, whose love of
words and reading rival my

own.

For Kieran Benjamin Ryan—you are
the most magical thing that has ever
happened to me. You have always been
my first dream, my greatest joy. I'm
so proud of
you.

Chapter 1

Frederick

The Town of Fairshaw, England, 1848

"The man who pockets the silver key
Hung on the collar of the Fairshaw Cat,
The same will be Master of Fairshaw.
Unimaginable riches, unparalleled power,
The Fairshaw bride and Fairshaw lands,
Be his alone."

And if I could twist fate's arm just right, that man would be me. The prophecy reverberated through my skull the same way it had rang out in the quiet of Rupert's pub days ago. But it no longer sounded with the croak of the old man who'd spoken then—the words were in my own voice, as if they, and the power they spoke of, were alive inside my brain.

"The magic of words fills the air of the Library…" The schoolmaster's words had slurred as he'd come stumbling out of the dingy pub at day break. He'd hiccoughed and grabbed his friend's arm. "Even," another hiccough, "into the veins of the Library Master." Their uneven gait had carried them down the street as the clocktower's last chime rang out over the town, and my mind had spun with the possibilities.

What must it be like to have magic like that? Would it pound in my veins like a horse's hooves against the cobblestones before a speeding hackney? Shimmer through my bloodstream like sunlight on frosted rooftops in winter? Would I know soon?

I reached out to touch the thick, leafy vine that crawled its way up the looming brick wall in front of me. The Library magic had released the cat the night Edward Fairshaw had passed, the same night I'd heard the prophecy. In the three days since, while the good citizens of Fairshaw had veiled themselves in black, I'd tried to work out a plan to catch it. On Pendle Street we owned no mourning clothes, nor did we have the means to acquire them. And as for plans, I'd come up empty, other than with this.

My gaze trailed the vine as it rose towards the window far above me. I'd caught enough information from the lovestruck scholar I'd met at the pub, a frequent visitor to the Library, to assume the window halfway up this wall to be Adelaide Fairshaw's.

Wouldn't the washer women, gossiping as they pegged strangers' shirts onto fraying clothes lines, have a field day if a Holloway became the Fairshaw Master? I grinned. *Sure they would, and then they'd go right back to fussing over some other washed-up dock trash.*

And, they could regale each other with embellished tales of my adventures all they wanted. It didn't matter to *them* that my perseverance had left me nothing but a dinged reputation—seldom the coins needed to feed my sisters. But that would all change if I became the Fairshaw Master. The Fairshaw Library's stately manor would be my home, and the town and woods surrounding it would all be mine. *I'd be a wealthy man.*

My pulse raced at the thought of bringing my older sister a bag full of coins. She'd no longer have to scrape the mold off the sides of her bread. My younger sister wouldn't need to serve as a maid at the Library to earn her keep. She could play in the streets by day and be tucked in at night by someone who'd counted her first steps—like all children ought to.

I hooked an arm over the first branch of the vine and tugged. It seemed sturdy enough. In my best suit of clothes and a top hat left behind by some toff that'd visited Rupert's pub, I'd dressed far better than my social standing. Martha always said that clothes made the man. I hoped she was right, and that fine clothes would be enough to convince Edward Fairshaw's daughter to spill her secrets.

I pulled myself up, finding a foothold on a brick jutting out a foot off the ground. My conscience twitched. Eerily absent for so long, it had certainly chosen an inconvenient time to come knocking. But I needed to do this. For myself, yes, but also for the two souls who relied on me.

My hand searched for another bare piece of vine. There. I slid my hand under a cluster of leaves and clamped my arm around it, then braced my knee on the curved branch.

The Library manor was known for the spells guarding it. Was the vine I climbed magical too? I felt no spark of magic under my hands, only rough wood and silken leaves. *Perhaps just a common plant.*

I kept my gaze on the windowsill far above me as I moved and pictured the look on Martha's face if she ever found out I'd climbed the wall to visit the Fairshaw's daughter. I chuckled. My sister would be unimpressed, but while she might give me a verbal bashing, I doubted she'd care once I was the Fairshaw. And I would become the Fairshaw—I had to.

I gripped another branch of vine and pushed away from my foothold, repeating the series of movements as the ground fell away below me. Finally, my fingers hooked around the square beam at the bottom of the frame. I slid my boots along the brick wall to find a place to rest my feet while I figured out how to go about this visit. Finding a foothold, I straightened.

The window was open.

I knew I couldn't enter the library—if gossip could be trusted, a spell kept unwanted guests out. Leaning closer, I felt the pulsing energy against my body. *Definitely a spell.*

I braced my weight on either side of the wide shutters, ignored the sting of magic, and lifted my head. My chin dropped at the sight that met me.

Miss Fairshaw stood facing away from me, her hair unbound, and only a dressing gown draping her tempting curves. Golden ringlets cascaded down her back as she leaned forward to touch her fingertips to the surface of the water in the large copper bathtub—as if she couldn't judge its temperature from the rising swirls of heat.

It was no secret that whoever found the cat would also find himself married to the Fairshaw's daughter, but I wasn't in this hunt for a bride.

Or, I hadn't been.

I swallowed hard, and leaned more of my weight into

the arm resting on the windowsill. Tilting my head, I watched my soon-to-be bride. I ought to look away—Martha had imprinted enough sense into my thick skull. But this woman drew and bound my attention with invisible strings.

The lady set to inherit Edward Fairshaw's great library didn't need beauty—she could've been a wizened, old hag, and still the most sought after bride in town. Was it magic that made her so compelling? She'd been born a Fairshaw, so surely the deep magic ran in her veins. Would it be visible on her bare skin? *If I didn't avert my eyes, I'd know soon.*

Shaking the water droplets off her fingers, she moved to loosen the tasseled cord around her waist. My conscience shuddered again, but I didn't heed it, nor did I drop my eyes from the mesmerizing scene in front of me. My pulse kicked up a notch as her dressing gown slipped lower, revealing her shoulders, the small of her back—my conscience finally got the better of me, and I averted my gaze.

A choked scream sounded, and I turned to see what she must have—my face reflected in the mirror behind the tub.

"What in the blazes do you think you're doing?" She clutched her dressing gown closed and whirled on me. Her eyes sparked with anger as her curses filled the room.

Raised among the rougher-edged ranks of society, you'd think I'd heard worse, but this toff's daughter made my ears burn. Her mouth twisted. "How dare you! Have you no decency?"

My lips stretched into a smirk. "Very little, I'm afraid."

Her nostrils flared, and she lunged as if to attack. I shifted away from her on instinct, remembering at the last minute I stood on a vine twelve feet in the air. A single step backward would send me plummeting to the ground—not the way I wanted to lose my chance at becoming Fairshaw Master.

Her eyes shone with triumph, and annoyance filled my chest. Had I just shrunk away from a lady, not only smaller than myself, but half-naked to boot? Anger slipped into my voice. "I didn't see anything that won't be my due as your husband, so there's no damage done."

"Husband." She scoffed, derision dripping from her voice. "You think *you* can catch the Fairshaw Cat?"

I'd heard it was feral, and I had no clue how to catch it. I'd come here for that very reason—hoping Miss Fairshaw might help me. After a first impression like this, it seemed unlikely. "I have no doubt I can catch your cat."

"And your plan is what, sir…?"

As if I'd tell her. "I'm Frederick Holloway, and I don't share my plans, only my intentions."

"To marry me?" She laughed without mirth. "You thought the best way to endear yourself to your future bride was to sneak up on her bathing? Like a Peeping-Tom?" Her spiteful voice rankled as much as her irreverence.

It was obvious she wasn't the most wanted woman in town for her sweetness. "Don't flatter yourself. I didn't know you were about to bathe when I climbed up here."

"It wasn't apparent when I began disrobing?" An angry flush spread across her cheekbones as her voice rose.

"On the contrary, Miss." I grinned remembering the creamy skin I'd glimpsed before I'd averted my gaze. Her eyes shone with something akin to hatred, and she called me another name fit to make a sailor blush.

I shifted my boots on the thick branch holding my weight. Miss Fairshaw might be a beauty. Her speech? Not so much. My time would be better spent on strategies for the cat hunt—it was time to leave.

"It's been lovely making your acquaintance, Miss Fairshaw, but I believe I have a cat to track down. Until next time." I tipped the brim of my top hat and, to the sound of her angry voice, dropped from the windowsill.

CHAPTER 2

Adelaide

Shock kept me motionless too long. When I finally ran to the window and leaned out, the man who'd called himself Frederick Holloway was turning the corner of the bakery across the street. He must have all but slid down the knobbly vine to escape that fast!

Admiration flickered in my chest. If he wasn't such a cad, I'd have asked him where he'd learned to climb like that. Except that he'd come upon me half-naked, without attempting to make himself known—proof he was the worst sort of man. Seething, I slammed the shutters and snapped the lock in place. I called him another dirty name and hoped his palms were nothing but splinters.

How could I have known that the spell that kept outsiders out didn't keep them from peeking through the windows? Had my father ever considered that the wall to my room could be scaled? *Would he have cared?*

I doubted it. I'd never known the man Edward Fairshaw had been before he'd lost my mother, only the shell of a man he'd been since.

I glanced toward the window to make sure I was alone before I let my dressing gown fall to the floor. I sank into the bath. The hot water enveloped me, and I pressed down the surge of emotion rising in my chest. *I was a pawn in a competition meant to find a man fit to wield unlimited power—there was no room for silly emotions.* I closed my eyes, trying to shut out my anxious thoughts, but the pressure beneath my ribs remained.

The Fairshaw Cat had roamed the surrounding lands for three days. I'd spent those same hours pushing the truth to the back of my mind, but now that I'd met a man who already considered me his property I could no longer keep it at bay.

I sank under the surface of the water, wishing I could stay forever. Alas, my lungs screamed for air long before I was ready to leave the dim underwater world. I broke the surface gasping for breath.

I hadn't given much thought to what kind of husband I'd get once he found the key. A girl needed a husband whether she wanted one or not, and I'd never expected to have a say in the decision. But meeting Mr. Holloway had cracked open the shell of my nonchalance.

Rising from the water—again making sure mine were the only set of eyes in the room—I wrapped myself in a towel. I glanced at the window. Still shut.

Images of his smirking face teased my brain. Had I watched him from afar, I wouldn't have balked at the thought of marrying him. His broad shoulders and boyish smile must get him plenty of female attention. But his lack of remorse over watching me undress and his hungry eyes as he spoke of finding the cat? I wasn't sure I could live with those.

Sure, he'd retreated when I'd lunged at the window—idiocy on my part since the spell made it impossible to enter the manor without a Fairshaw's invitation, which I certainly hadn't extended. But his swift retreat could have been instinct. *If we were married there wouldn't be a brick wall between us.*

I shuddered and closed my eyes. I wanted to forget about Mr. Holloway, but his infuriating smirk and glittering dark eyes seemed plastered to the inside of my eyelids.

A knock at the door startled me.

"Enter?"

A maid stepped inside, her gaze on the tips of her shoes. "M'lady. The minister has arrived and is being shown to his rooms. Elizabeth asked me to help you dress."

I groaned and pressed my fingertips into the space

between my brows to relieve the ache there. How could I have forgotten that the minister was supposed to arrive to-day? *One more piece in place for my imminent wedding.* "Oh. Yes, of course, Lydia."

I sank to the bed and watched as the maid placed the dark gown over a chair. She looked up, finally meeting my eyes. "Would you like me to dry your hair, M'lady? I would have found you sooner, but I…" Her cheeks pinked. "I was delayed, M'lady."

I smiled. "Don't worry about it, Lydia. And, yes, that would be fine."

"Thank you, M'lady." She curtsied and went about her duties. The blush in her cheeks confirmed my suspicions about her delay. Just yesterday, I'd entered what I'd thought was an empty room, only to find her kissing a male servant.

I'd tiptoed out, making sure they didn't see me. Edward Fairshaw would have notified his housekeeper and threatened to fire them, but I was not my father. I didn't care if a servant wanted to court another. If anything, I was jealous. What would it be like to be free to marry whoever you pleased? And why did a simple housemaid have more agency in her life than the daughter of a gentleman? My shoulders heaved on a sigh.

"M'lady, are you all right?" Lydia patted my shoulder.

"We all mourn your father. You are not alone in your grief."

Was I not? They'd seen how my father had treated me all my years, and yet they expected me to grieve him? If my face was lined with grief, it was for my own loss of freedom, not the death of my father. Anger tumbled hot and sharp through my blood, and I pressed my lips together as I blinked away fresh tears. Lydia's sympathetic gaze met mine in the mirror.

Why couldn't I be allowed to spend my days gaining knowledge and overseeing the running of the Fairshaw estate? It was an acceptable way of life for every blasted scholar that frequented these halls, but not for me? I was certain my father could have waived the stipulations of my inheritance before his death, so why had he insisted I marry? I wiped my tears and huffed out a breath. "Why can't the Fairshaw Master be a woman?"

The towel massaging my head stilled. "Are you asking me, M'lady?"

Guilt pinged my heart at Lydia's startled face looking back at me in the mirror. "I'm sorry. No, Lydia, I was just thinking out loud. Please carry on." I knew better than to question what Edward Fairshaw did or why. If he'd had any qualms about leaving his only child at the mercy of a stranger whose sole claim to respect was catching a half-feral house cat, he'd never shown it.

I was under no delusion that the men of Fairshaw were hunting for the cat on my behalf. The prize they sought was the Library and its promise of unsurpassed power, magic, and knowledge. I was but the whipped cream—my worth would melt away as my youth faded. *And all that time I'd be at the mercy of a stranger.*

I wanted to ditch my towel, crawl under the sheets, and let the scent of sunshine on fresh linens push away my dark future. If not for Lydia's presence, I would have. Instead, I stood and let her help me dress. Another hideous gown made from black parramatta silk. Even while in mourning, I had responsibilities as the Mistress of the Library. I had a minister to greet, one who would soon tie me for life to a man I didn't love and who wouldn't love me.

Maybe even the one who'd so recklessly climbed the wall of my home today. I shivered as his dark gaze pressed into my mind again. I'd seen no desire for me there, only for power. Power-hungry men were always ruthless, that much my magical library had taught me.

Whoever my husband was, he wouldn't remain unknown for long. From what I'd read, marriage wasn't a place where boundaries remained. Physical ones at least. Emotionally, I might be forever married to a stranger.

Lydia gave my bodice one last tug, and at her nod, I

turned in a circle. "You are all ready, M'lady. I'll have, um, Shepherd come in and remove the water in your tub." She didn't sound as annoyed as Elizabeth did at my insisting on taking my baths the old-fashioned way. But then Elizabeth didn't have a sweetheart ready to empty my cooled water either.

"Thank you, Lydia."

I put a trembling hand on my door handle. I hated the feel of the scratchy crape against my wrists as much as the forced emotion it signaled. As if my grief for a man who'd never cared for me could be called forth by wearing proper mourning clothes. Anger surged again. *I was the wealthiest woman in all of Fairshaw, and yet, I wouldn't get to choose who entered my life, or my bed.* I couldn't mourn the man who'd put me in this position.

I pulled in a deep breath, trying to calm myself. I would pray Mr. Holloway didn't have what it took to find the cat—it was the only action left to me. Opening the door, I schooled my expression. I would have time to think about the misery of my existence later. For now, I needed to act the charming hostess. If only charm could raise a man from the dead and make him change his mind.

CHAPTER 3

Frederick

My muscles ached as I pushed the last crate on top of the knotted ropes on the ground. The stench of rotting wood and week-old sweat assaulted my senses, and the shouts of men and squawking of gulls filled the air.

"Haul away!" The ropes strained as they tightened around the crates. Pulleys groaned as the load lifted off the ground, swinging on its way up. This part of the cargo, at least, was checked and loaded. Soon it would be on its way to a foreign port far away from England, where it would make some wealthy merchant more money.

The overseer didn't quiet, and a handful of dockworkers scurried to fulfill the orders he hollered into the air. But I was done for the day. Judging by the grunt from the worker next to me, I wasn't the only one who'd reached my limit. We shared a look and together made our way over to the line of workers waiting to be paid. The worker's clothes were as worn as my own—whatever gold these goods brought, it wouldn't be lining our pockets. *Nor would it feed our families.*

Liv's pale face flashed in my mind, her dark eyes wide with fear as Martha explained she'd need to go serve at the Fairshaw Library. The memory tightened my gut. The girl had been orphaned as an infant, and the mere thought of her enduring the backbreaking labor of a house servant caused bile to rise in my throat. *If I had done better, she could have stayed with Martha. With me.*

"Hey, mate! Line's moving." A grumbled curse and a shove to my back pulled me out of my dark thoughts. I sent the man a scowl and moved forward. If the ache in my shoulders hadn't felt like the yoke it was, I'd have given him a shove in return.

"Good thing for his sister that she's prettier than this bloke, or she'd not have as many visitors come evening, would she?"

And *there* was my motivation. I rounded on the speaker and sunk my fist into his jaw. He dropped to the ground, but his mate delivered a punch to my shoulder that reverberated through my bones.

At the head of the line a burly man whistled and waved his arms. "Hey, break it up lads! Take your coin and go." I sent a half-hearted punch in the direction of the second lad, now leaning over his buddy on the ground, then turned to get my payment.

"Your name?"

"Holloway." The man scratched down a snarled script illegible to me, and handed me an amount that would barely get us supper. I stepped out of line and turned towards the street I'd grown up on. One where most men stayed until the day they died, struggling through a life not fit to live like their parents before them. I wanted more than that.

I stretched my stiff neck and groaned. I'd go home and sleep an hour before I began trawling the woods for my ticket out of this misery—a cat that would bring me enough riches to get my little sister out of servanthood.

The tug at my waist took me by surprise, then the sound of ripping fabric tore the air. *Damn it!* Another thing on my plate tonight. "Think you'll get to walk away from a fight, do you?" Before I could turn to see his face, pain radiated from a hit to my kidney. I whirled on the same guy I'd sent to the ground earlier. His wide grin showed rotted stumps where his teeth had once been. "Thought I'd pay you a visit on the way to see your sister."

I smashed my hand into his mouth, ignoring the pain that radiated through my knuckles. His yelp was more than worth it. "As if my sister would ever look twice at the likes of you." He spat on the ground. Bright red mixed with a black, tar-like substance. His curses filled the air.

I snarled. "Had enough, or do you want a black-eye too? Might make a girl feel sorry enough for you to give you some attention." His insult was lost in his growl, but he didn't move forward.

"I thought so." I turned and walked away, ears peeled for movement from behind. But I'd given him whatever fight he'd needed out of his system. And for it, I had a torn shirt. One my sister would make me mend myself.

"Why are you limping?" Martha's dark eyes reminded me so much of our mother the old ache tugged in my chest. The woman who'd given birth to us had worked herself into an early grave, but she'd never had to send us away. *Like I had with Liv.* I shoved the pained thought down, ignoring it like I tried to ignore my throbbing shoulder.

"Idiots at the docks."

She rolled her eyes and scraped a pitiful amount of porridge into the bowl on the table. "Can you never stay out of fights?"

I wanted to deny it, but it wasn't the first time I'd arrived home limping. "I...often stay out of fights. When I can." I didn't need to turn around to know she'd directed another eyeroll at me, but I did. "That idiot Bill Davis was running his mouth about you again. You aren't…friendly with him, are you?"

Martha's face turned so red that I retreated a step. "Frederick James Holloway, you better take that back right now!" She shuddered, but the anger in her eyes didn't dissipate. "I can't believe you'd think that! You didn't confirm it, did you?"

It was my turn to roll my eyes. "Not by a long shot. I beat him up."

She groaned. "So now it will look like you tried to defend me, and people will talk."

I couldn't believe this. "You're angry with me for defending your honor?"

She pressed two fingers into the space between her eyebrows, a sure sign she was trying to keep her irritation in check. "His mother hasn't ever heard a piece of gossip and not passed it on. You know as well as I do that she'll take this and run with it."

"Anyone who knows you will know it's a lie! The only women Bill can get are the ones he has to pay after." Before, if they had any inkling of the kind of man he was.

"Anyone who knows Liv is employed by the Library at her age will know we're suffering for money. They'll draw their own conclusions." The truth of her words was like another kick to my kidney. Martha would never blame me for our lack of funds, if anything, she blamed herself. But the guilt choked me. The nap I'd longed for could wait. If I wanted to keep my sisters from a fate like our mother's, I'd use this last hour of daylight to search for the cat.

I shoveled a few bites of food into my mouth, knowing my sister would eat whatever I left behind, and shrugged a coat over my ripped shirt. Mending it could wait. Everything could wait—I needed to find that cat yesterday.

"How does a man even catch this cat? Did the prophecy ever say anything about that?" I turned to the man voicing my very thoughts. If you could call him a man. Under the filth on his face, he looked younger than me, maybe sixteen, if that. His friend, leaning his scrawny elbow against the door jamb of the shabby building behind me, couldn't be much older.

Why hadn't Edward Fairshaw thought to put an age limit on the man who'd marry his daughter? Miss Fairshaw had to be a half a decade older than these lanky boys. I tried to picture her reaction if either of them won the game her father had set up. She'd probably have him cowering at the other end of the room while her temper flared.

I grinned, then stepped forward and stumbled over a bowl that reeked of rotted fish. Righting myself, I turned to see an older woman jump up from the overturned bucket by the brick wall. "Watch your step! Did you spill it? He didn't spill it, did he, Tommy? Tommy!" She shouted the last word, and a half-dressed man stumbled drunkenly out from the darkened interior of their house. He looked wildly around. "He spill the potion, Ma?"

I took another step away from the bowl of greenish brown liquid, and tried to keep my supper from coming back up. "You're trying to attract the Fairshaw Cat with that?" I gagged as another whiff hit my nostrils.

The woman straightened, a note of pride in her voice. "Old Molly swears it'll bring the cat right up to our door-step, she said. We'll just have to sit and watch for it. Old Molly knows her trade, see, she raised Tommy here from the dead when he was a child. Dead as a doornail, he was."

I raised an eyebrow. I couldn't blame Old Molly. She was likely desperate for the coins she'd wrung out of this woman's shallow pockets. But I doubted the foul liquid would help the woman in front of me secure her son's future.

The clocktower chimed through town, and I moved

along the street, desperate for the clean air of the woods. I'd spent the last hour trawling the streets adjacent to the docks and had found several cats, but not one with a collar, much less a silver key. *Soon it would be dark, and I'd be out of time.* I passed the blacksmith's forge and followed the hard stamped dirt trail through the tall grass.

Blessedly fresh air filled my lungs as I stepped into the dark space between the pines. Was the cat smart enough to avoid the streets of Fairshaw? What were the chances it simply hid in the woods until the frenzied search calmed?

I pursed my lips around the smacking sound I'd once used to get the attention of the scrawny tabby Martha had taken pity on when we were children. She'd let it lick her bowl clean after dinner once, and it had lurked around the corners of our house for years after. But that had been back when our mother's even stitches from daybreak to nightfall had kept food on our table. Martha and I both worked now, and it still hadn't been enough to keep Liv home—not when her meager meals could be provided at the Library.

I searched the area around me, but it was no use. What passed for twilight in town was utter blackness between the trees. Would it be worth the walk down to Rupert's pub to hear if there were any new sightings?

Leaves rustled close by, and I crouched to the ground.

23

"Here, kitty." An animal scurried away from me, but it wasn't big enough to be a cat. A bushy, red tail trailed up a tree. I let out a sigh. A squirrel solved exactly none of my problems.

Chapter 4

Frederick

Striding down the wet, shiny cobblestones of Main Street in the dark, my thoughts were much the same hue as the night around me. I was no closer to finding the damned cat than I'd been a week ago. Holloways didn't admit defeat, but if we did, I'd be close. I shoved my hands into my trouser pockets, and kicked at a rock.

I could go see Miss Fairshaw again, but what good would that do? She wasn't connected to her family cat any more than I was to the tabby that licked the watered-down milk from our dirt floor after one of Liv's mishaps. Then again, *our cat wasn't magic,* like the Fairshaw Cat. Like Miss Fairshaw.

I slowed my walk. Perhaps I'd been wrong to dismiss her usefulness. Was she the clue I'd sought all along? I turned and strode through the streets until I stood at the foot of the thick vine I now knew for sure led to her window. She'd all but attacked me four days ago. I wasn't sure

I'd be any better received this time, but I wouldn't know if I didn't try.

Gripping the slippery vine with both hands, I hauled myself up. The last time had been an easy climb, but tonight my slick boot soles slid across the wet wood and my hands slipped along the wood until splinters stabbed my palms.

I considered turning around—more than once—but I wasn't a Holloway for nothing. I had my family pride, and my reputation for perseverance was well-earned. *I wasn't giving up now.*

Sweat trickled down my spine underneath my thread-bare shirt as I neared the dim light of her window. I paused, my head a foot below the windowsill. Now what? Should I knock? Risk her seeing me peep at her window again?

"Did you ever consider knocking at the front door and giving your calling card to Stonier?" Miss Fairshaw's voice, dripping with derision, sounded from somewhere above my head, and I almost lost my grip on the vine. Tilting my head, I found her above me, perched on a branch thicker than her waist.

Anger surged in my chest. "What are you doing out here? The vines are slick from the rain, you could break your neck climbing around on them!" Her recklessness

26

was appalling! How could she take so little care for her life? And, better yet, why did *I* care? She was nothing to me.

Miss Fairshaw scoffed. "You don't think you're in somewhat of a precarious position to be scolding *me* for climbing wet branches?"

"Not the same. I'm a grown man and you're—"

"I think it would be in your favor not to finish that sentence." The fire I'd seen in her eyes that first day must not be out of character. It sparked in her voice now—not the reception I'd hoped for. *Then perhaps you should have begun with a less volatile statement.*

I toed another vine for a place to push off. Once I found a firm foothold, I lifted my gaze again. "My apologies, Miss, I didn't mean—"

"Yes, you did."

I narrowed my eyes. "Have you ever been taught that it's rude to interrupt?"

"Have *you* ever been taught it's rude to climb up a person's wall when they would have turned you away at the door?"

I hoisted myself onto another thick branch.

She would, without a doubt, have turned me away at the door, or made her butler do so for her, but her careless behavior rankled more than the dismissal.

Level with her perch, I gave her a hard stare. "Have you given any thought to the fact that you're out alone after nightfall, easy prey for any madman strolling the streets in the dark?"

She blanched, and her eyes widened. "Is that a threat?"

The slight tremble in her voice was enough to make me feel like a cad. "What? No, of course not." Her silence was all but an accusation. "Why would I come up here to threaten you?"

Her pale throat worked. "I don't know why you'd come up here at all, to be honest." *Neither did I.* Her hostility at our last meeting had made it clear she didn't want to see me again. I'd had no reason to believe this call would be cordial.

"Is it so impossible to believe that I'm here to talk to you?"

"Why should I believe you?" The tremble remained in her voice, and I wanted to kick myself for frightening her.

A cool night breeze swept past, chilling the places where sweat had left my skin damp. "I didn't come up here to harm you. I came to"—I searched for the words—"offer my friendship." The furthest thing from my mind when I'd begun my climb towards her window now seemed like an excellent idea.

I swung up onto the branch where she sat, leaving our

28

bodies mere feet apart. Her gasp filled the air around us. "What are you doing?"

"I'm sitting on a branch of library vine with my friend." I patted the rough bark next to me, enjoying her ire a little too much. I took a deep breath of fresh air, so different from the rotting stench by the docks.

"She's not your friend! I mean, *I'm* not your friend. And *library vine* isn't a thing."

"What do you call it?"

"Uninvited, intrusive stranger."

I rolled my eyes and nodded to the cluster of leaves draping the wall at my side. "I meant the vine."

"Oh." She tugged her lip between her teeth, and I pulled my eyes away from the alluring sight lest she'd think I was leering at her. *Again.* "It's a honeysuckle."

She kept a straight face, but she was lying through her teeth—on Pendle Street you learned to discern the truth from a lie before you learned to run. And even if not, I would have recognized the reeking bush that had grown through the trash littering the curbside by our house. Whatever name the plant we sat on bore before it gripped the Fairshaw Library's magical brick walls, it wasn't honeysuckle. "It's not."

Surprise lit her features. "It's a Humulus lupulus."

Did she think her use of its latin name would trip me

up? I raised an eyebrow. "Hops? Like the ones used to brew beer?"

"One and the same." She met my suspicion with a smile much too sweet for what I knew of her personality. Or was she more sweet-tempered than she let on? Perhaps a friendship with Miss Fairshaw wouldn't be so unpleasant. I could think of better things than marrying an enemy.

I slid my hand along the vine stretching over our heads, and my gaze followed. "I didn't know hops grew like this."

"They don't. Except along the walls of this library."

I'd always wondered why they called it "the Library" when they could have simply called it "the manor." It made no sense. Was anything surrounding this building what it seemed like at first sight? Was the lady beside me? I turned to find her eyes on me, a frown marring her pretty forehead. It smoothed the instant she realized she had my attention. Shuttered blue eyes met mine for a second before she dropped her gaze.

The great clock chimed, the sound much louder here than at the docks. Miss Fairshaw lifted her head towards the sound. When the last chime rang through the stillness, neither of us spoke as we watched the sleeping town spread out beneath us. The creaks of wooden signs sway-ing on hooks in the breeze made their way up to our perch. Below them, winding cobblestone streets looked like shining veins between the townhouses, and gas lamps tossed light into puddles turned lakes of liquid gold.

Sitting next to Miss Fairshaw on a vine far above town as the sounds of evening and her soft breathing washed over me, felt a lot like peace. I hadn't climbed the vine tonight expecting to find peace. Not with her.

I shifted to find a more comfortable seat. She stiffened as if I'd cracked a whip. Annoyance rattled the stillness in-side me. "Why are you afraid of me?"

She hesitated, then her voice came softly. "You're easily twice my size." She glanced down at my hand resting on the vine between us, and swallowed. "Strong enough to snap me in half if you wanted to. The first time we met, you gloated at the thought of possessing my body. Alone with you here in the dark, why wouldn't I be afraid of you?"

I rarely felt shame, but at these words—from a woman whose opinion I hadn't known I valued—the withering emotion spread in my chest. Had I really given her the im-pression that I'd harm her? "I owe you an apology, Miss Fairshaw. Yes, I plan to know you like a husband knows his wife once we are that, but don't think for a moment

I'd ever use that desire to hurt you. Or take anything you didn't want to give."

Her mouth dropped open. "You're mocking me."

The hurt in her whisper hit me like a slap. Hadn't I just apologized? Why did she insist on seeing me as a villain? "I'm not mocking you. I don't know what you've heard of me, but whoever told it didn't know me."

She snorted. "Your determination to win any prize you set your mind to is a lie?"

As if the two were remotely the same. Did this woman speak in anything but riddles? "I never said that. But it doesn't mean I would harm you. Married or not."

She straightened beside me. "My servants would never lie to me."

"But they listen to gossip and repeat it."

"It isn't gossiping if it's true."

My eyebrows rose. Did she really believe that? "I'd expect a bit more astuteness from a woman raised in the Fairshaw Library."

Her eyes snapped. "I expect nothing from a man raised on the docks."

The old prejudice rankled. No matter the finery I put on, or the care I took to refine my speech, I could never outrun my birthplace. Would I always be the Holloway from Pendle Street? "So you think I'm a cad?"

She raised an eyebrow. "Shouldn't I?" Her words were haughty, as if the air she breathed next to me was more valuable than that entering my lungs. But she was wrong. I might never rise beyond Pendle Street, but at least I didn't think it gave me a right to thread on those who had even less than me.

"You could easily best the filthiest mouth I've heard in old Rupert's pub; I don't know that birthplace means much." My words were scathing enough I knew she'd rise to my bait.

"You filthy—"

"Don't poison the night air with your dirty mouth. You've proven my point. You aren't high-bred or wise from all your exposure to nobility and knowledge. And maybe I'm not such an ill-bred thief and drunkard even if raised to be one."

I pushed myself up from the vine. I was done with this. I needed to figure out how to catch the cat. Once I got that far, I'd have all the time in the world to resign myself to a life with this spitfire. Tonight, I'd had enough.

CHAPTER 5

Adelaide

"Have you heard the news?" Elizabeth's eyes sparkled as she lowered her overflowing tray of food. Technically my lady's maid, she was also the closest thing I had to a sister.

For the last eight days, every piece of news she'd brought had been about the Fairshaw Cat or the men hunting for it. I hoped this was something else. I'd rather hear about milk prices—factory strikes in London!—anything but the Fairshaw Cat. I dropped my book into my lap. "What news is that?"

Excitement lit her expression, and she pushed at the wispy strands of brown that had escaped her tiny white cap. "Frederick Holloway is searching for the Fairshaw Cat!"

I shuddered. *Did I ever know.*

"Are you cold?" Elizabeth lowered the tray to the table, grabbed another of the horrid black crape shawls, and ignored my protests as she wrapped it around my shoulders. "Tsk. I saw you shiver, don't lie to me. You sat outside in the damp evening air again, didn't you? I understand your need to get away, but could you at least bring a shawl?"

"Yes, mother. I'll try." I rolled my eyes. Unfazed, Elizabeth poured my tea and plopped onto my bed—servant's duties entirely forgotten. Not that there would be consequences. My father had preached time and again about the proper relationship between servant and master, but I didn't care. And until there was a new Fairshaw Master, my word was the one that counted.

I closed my book and tossed it towards my nightstand. The thick volume hit the hardwood floor with a thud and a flutter of pages. "So why is this Holloway man news?"

"He's quite the handsome rogue. Rumor has it the ladies of Fairshaw are dropping like flies." Elizabeth gave a dramatic sigh, slapped the back of her hand against her forehead and fell to the mattress in a mock faint.

I laughed. "Elizabeth! Surely he's not the only man in Fairshaw worthy of that description?"

She blinked an eye open. "He's also known for his determination." *Just like Lydia had said when I'd quizzed her.* A chill slithered down my spine. What would become of me at the mercy of a man like that? "What if he's cruel?"

Bedding rustled behind me, and Elizabeth sat up. "I haven't heard anyone call him that, only that the dictionary has his picture next to *perseverance*." I had access to every dictionary ever written, and while there might be a picture of Mr. Holloway somewhere in one of them, it wasn't under *perseverance*. Could he really find the cat?

"So all he's got going for him is that he's handsome and insistent?"

"Like a dog with a bone." Elizabeth winked. I didn't care for being this man's newest bone and said as much. But instead of bowing to reason, she frowned. "If you have to marry a random stranger, wouldn't you rather he be handsome?"

"No, I'd rather he be kind." *And honorable and faithful.* You didn't grow up in a magic library, breathing in stories old and new every day for all your years without touching on tales of love. Sacrificial love, undying love, romantic love. But none of those would be my fate.

Elizabeth tsked. "Only kind? What about love?"

"What *about* love?" I sighed, ignored the scent of perfectly brewed Earl Grey that wafted up from the teapot, and bent to grab my discarded book from the floor.

Her frown deepened. "You want a husband who doesn't love you?"

"Of course I don't. But there's no use wanting what you

can't have. And I know for a fact that Mr. Holloway wouldn't love me."

Suspicion filled her eyes. "How could you know? Have you met him?" I locked my gaze on the bookshelf across the room, not wanting her to read the truth in my eyes.

"You honestly think the man who'll catch a magic cat to possess the power of the great Library will love me?" I sniffed. "He'd be a power hungry beast, probably not able to love at all. I don't anticipate being able to turn a mind that twisted."

"What if he wasn't twisted, but simply determined?"

I raised an eyebrow. "The cat has the Fairshaw magic on its side. It's not a housecat, Bets."

"*Adelaide.*" Her voice was full of reproach. "Being skillful and cunning doesn't mean one isn't capable of love." She scooted closer and wrapped her arm around my shoulders. She gestured to the tray in front of me. "Are you not going to eat?"

I shook my head. "I'm not hungry." Who could think of food with the prospect of a husband like Mr. Holloway? I was barely twenty-one, and the rest of my life stretched before me like an endless row of demands from a man I didn't know. Would my husband rule like my father had? Let his studies consume his life and only ever seek me out when I failed his expectations? Or would he do worse?

"But you'll have tea?" It wasn't a question. I was going to have tea whether I wanted to or not. If I didn't, Elizabeth would worry. She might talk to the house-keeper, and I didn't want to explain to the robust woman why the thought of marrying a stranger made my stomach turn. Mrs. Tabor would understand, but I didn't want to chance any sage advice she might have for me. If it was anything like the snippet of "marital advice" she'd given me the morning the cat had been released, I was certain it would *permanently* damage my appetite.

"Thank you." I wrapped my fingers around the teacup and took a sip. The sharp flavor coated my tongue. Had she left the leaves in the pot as we'd talked? She must have.

A crash sounded from the servant's stairs hidden be-hind the papered wall, and Elizabeth's hand flew to cover her mouth. "That's Livvie. I'm training her. I need to go." Wide-eyed she sprang from the bed and disappeared through the near-invisible wallpapered door. And I was left with my bitter tea and a lump of dread in my stomach.

CHAPTER 6

Frederick

The branch I'd held snapped back, and wet pine needles slapped my face. I let out another curse as the freezing water trickled down my face and neck to slide inside my shirt collar. I hadn't thought I'd had any dry skin left, but the cold drops found it. *You'd think as thick as the trees grew in these woods the branches would hold off some of the heavy drizzle from overhead. But no.*

I fought my way through the brush, soaked to the skin, while the scent of wet earth and spicy sap saturated the air. *Curse Edward Fairshaw and his idiotic ways of finding an heir!*

My plan to lure the cat's whereabouts from Miss Fairshaw had failed miserably. Either she truly didn't know, or she was more devious than she let on. I imagined if she had known where the cat could be found, she'd have gloated over the fact that she was keeping it from me, and she wasn't.

And so, I was left to trail the woodlands surrounding the town in this miserable downpour. A quiet rustle sounded to my left, and I halted. Could it be the cat? I stood unmoving, not wanting to startle the creature in case it was the one I sought. Twigs broke as it moved through the woods. If this was the cat it had to be massive. A deer?

But the dark shadow that pushed through the brush, so close I could have reached out to touch him, belonged to a man, not a beast. I caught a glimpse of his bushy eyebrows and sunken eyes and recognition flared through me.

Dr. Harrison's family had been healers in the town of Fairshaw for centuries, and they'd never suffered for money. But then the Fairshaw title held more than wealth for the man who caught the cat.

I waited for him to turn and notice me, but he didn't. I watched as he stepped out into the clearing and bent low to place several objects into the thick carpet of leaves, one following the other until the indentations in the leaves formed a crescent shape.

I squinted at the objects on the ground. They emitted a faint blue glow, almost as if... Was he trying to lure the cat out with magic? A hum sounded through the forest, like the purring of a feline, but louder. Dr. Harrison lifted his head in the direction of the sound, a triumphant smirk on his face. Then he lowered and gathered the glowing rocks into his purse, before he pushed his way through the underbrush toward the source of the vibration.

It should come as no surprise that Dr. Harrison dealt in magic as well as healing. That the Fairshaw family had old magic didn't mean they were the only ones. But what chance did I have against a man with magic on his side? If he had found the whereabouts of the cat, should I follow him? I shoved through the wet branches and stepped fully into the clearing. The hum in the air was loud enough to lead me in the right direction, still I hesitated. Something about this chance meeting set off warning bells in my head.

But I needed to find the Fairshaw Cat to secure my sisters' future, and I refused to give up. Until another man pressed the magical key into the lock of the Fairshaw Library, there was a chance—and I was going to fight for it. I moved through the brush, wincing as my old shoulder injury made itself known. The stabbing pain whenever the weather turned humid never failed to remind me I'd had to work too hard too young. I wouldn't let it happen to Liv for a moment longer than it already had. When I became the Fairshaw Master, she could get the rest and nourishment she needed.

The twin fires of blue that popped into my mind didn't belong to either of my sisters, and for a moment they slowed my steps. But if building a life with a woman who despised me was the price for providing for my family, I'd gladly pay it. I was going to find that cat—if it was the last thing I did.

Chapter 7

Adelaide

The light breeze shuttled the clouds across the sky above us and tested the hold of the elaborate coiffure Elizabeth had spent the better part of her morning on. Praying the hair pins would hold it secure, I surveyed the stalks of rhubarb in front of me. "Are these the only ones you have, Miss?"

"Yes, M'lady, Miss Fairshaw." The girl manning the booth hunched her shoulders, as if she could make herself small enough to escape my notice.

The fruit wasn't as fresh as I'd hoped, but the kitchen staff would still be able to use them for jams and tarts, wouldn't they? Rhubarb was versatile, and we could still use more desserts for the upcoming banquet. *The banquet where I'd be paraded around like fresh meat for the contestants of the hunt.* I shuddered, but when I spoke my voice was carefully scrubbed of dread. "Can you deliver the rhubarb to the Fairshaw Library, Miss? The housekeeper will make sure you get paid for your delivery." I pointed to the small fruit tarts in front of me. "I'd like to pay for these for myself, please."

She curtseyed, shoulders a little less hunched when she straightened. "Certainly, M'lady. How much of the rhubarb would you like?"

"I'll take all of it, please, Miss." The girl's eyes widened. She opened her mouth as if to protest, then wisely shut it again. I fiddled with my reticule and withdrew the funds for the tarts. A little more than the price she'd stated when I'd arrived.

She counted the coins and paused. "M'lady, they aren't this much."

"For your patience. I've kept you long enough." I smiled at the girl, careful not to let my eyes linger on the worn cuffs of her too small dress. Those extra coins would do her much more good than they ever would me. *Or my soon-to-be husband.*

Elizabeth sighed behind me as we turned away from the booth. "Adelaide, you aren't making a real difference by overpaying for day-old tarts at the market."

We'd had this conversation before. She didn't see my side of it, and maybe she never would. But *she* wasn't the one who'd been born to so much privilege it almost choked her. "With my father gone and no husband in his place, I'm not answering to anyone for what I spend."

If the cat was found tonight, this would be my last day of freedom. I wasn't going to let it slip by when I still had a chance to do good.

Her eyes softened, as if she knew where my mind had gone. "He might be a good husband, Adelaide."

I tucked an errant strand of hair back under my hat. *The pins hadn't held.* "There are no guarantees for that, is there?"

She didn't answer.

I tugged off a glove the color of death, bit into the tiny tart, and pushed away the despair at the edges of my mind. Two women, a booth over, tilted their heads together. Had I heard my father's name? I couldn't be sure. One woman's wide grin showed several missing teeth. She gestured in my direction, and I shivered. This was my first outing since the beginning of the hunt for the Fairshaw Cat, and these two weren't the first to scrutinize me today. The rowdy laughter grated, and I was glad I hadn't caught their full conversation. It was bad enough to be passed off to the winner of a game hunt, having every single person in town know somehow made it more humiliating.

My cheeks burned as I walked towards the end of the row of booths, desperately wanting to remove myself from their line of sight. The shouts of sellers rang through the air, joining the chatter from the buyers heckling prices. Drowning out the laughter that still echoed in my mind.

Out of nowhere, a dog sprinted across the road in front of me, so close it brushed my skirts. The child on its heels bumped me off balance. The wrapped tarts flew out of my hand as I flailed my arms wildly. I tipped forward, grasping for purchase and finding only air. I was going to fall on my face in front of every gossip in—

Strong hands gripped my waist, then my wrist, halting the filthy cobblestones in their rapid ascent toward me. My heart pounded in my chest, and I gasped for breath.

"Are you all right, M'lady?" Eyes as blue as a summer sky met mine, and my breath caught in my lungs for a completely different reason.

"Adelaide! M'lady, are you hurt?" Elizabeth's worried hands gripped mine, as the stranger stepped back. She straightened my hat and brushed at a black smudge on my wrist.

I drew in a deep breath and shook my head. "I'm fine, Elizabeth." I turned to my savior as he straightened from retrieving his cap from the cobbled street. "Thank you for your quick response Mr…"

"Nicholas Cromwell, M'lady, at your service." He gave an easy bow, and a grin appeared. He bent again to pick up the now crushed tarts and handed me the package.

"Are you sure you are well, M'lady?" Concern filled his eyes, and my heart tripped.

Why weren't the ladies of Fairshaw already flocking around us? How had they not noticed *this man*? "I'm certain I'm fine, thank you for your assistance, Sir."

"I will be returning to my duties, then, M'lady. Miss Masfield." He bowed again, and nodded to Elizabeth. I was about to ask how she knew my rescuer, when another man's glare caught my eye.

Mr. Holloway's dark scowl drew me like a beacon from the end of the street. Gone was his tophat and fine clothes. Dressed like the dock worker he probably was, his broad shoulders strained the fabric of his shirt, and filth and sweat coated his bare neck and muscled forearms. His gaze followed Mr. Cromwell's retreating form, but I could have sworn he'd directed it at me a second ago.

Then our eyes met, but no smile replaced his flinty expression. Without acknowledging my presence at all, he turned back to loading barrels into a wagon with the workers next to him. No one seeing our interaction would guess that we'd talked alone under cover of darkness just two nights ago. Which was just as well. I had no reason to have any more dealings with Mr. Holloway, and none at all for the flicker of disappointment under my ribs.

I turned my attention to Elizabeth. "How do you know Mr. Cromwell?"

"He's the blacksmith's son. Or rather the blacksmith as his father turned frail with an illness a year or so ago." That explained the width of his shoulders and the scent of fire and earth that had tinged the air around him. It didn't explain why Mr. Holloway had scowled at him, or me. *Did he have a score to settle with Mr. Cromwell? Were they both hunting for the cat?* The memory of sky blue eyes tugged at my heart, and I knew which suitor I'd pick if I had a choice.

"Are you ready to head home?" Elizabeth's voice pulled me out of my thoughts.

I brushed an invisible speck of dust off my dark skirts. "I'm very ready to leave the gossiping behind me."

She laughed. "I don't know that that will happen until you're good and married. As long as there's a chance of anyone they know catching the cat and becoming your husband, they won't stop wagging their tongues."

I groaned. "And you think they'll stop then?"

She shrugged. "Depending on who it is. If he's one of them, they might keep it up. And of course, depending on how he treats you, they'll spread whatever gossip escapes the Library, I imagine. Remember when—"

"Elizabeth! You're not making me feel any better!"

Her expression turned compassionate. "I'm sorry. I

wasn't trying to make you feel worse, M'lady." She glanced around to make sure we weren't being overheard. "Really, Adelaide, I wasn't."

"I know." I appreciated Elizabeth's friendship more than she could ever know, but my impending marriage didn't weigh her down like it did me.

The screech of a man's voice rang through the air. "Scum. Run back to the holes you crawled out of!"

A terrified scream muffled his next words, and then a little boy's voice rang clear through the air. "You mean toff! You're scaring my sister!"

Forgetting my station, I hurried around the corner. A man in a dark frock coat stood with lifted fist, crowding in on the three scrawny children cowering against the filthy brick wall of the school house. A little boy stood in front of the other two, eyes wide with fear, facing down the bully.

The gentleman shook his fist. "Did you hear what I said, gutter rat?" The boy paled under the grime. He looked ready to faint but didn't retreat. Admiration bubbled in my chest.

"What is going on here?" My words went unheeded, and I moved closer.

"Adelaide, don't—" Elizabeth tugged at my sleeve, but I pulled away and stepped forward.

I raised my voice, terrified of what might happen if I didn't. "I asked what is going on here!"

The little boy shifted his attention from the man in front of him, a glimmer of hope in his eyes as he turned them on me. "M'lady. I was simply asking this gentleman, here, if he could let us have a few coins for bread, and he— ouch!" Tears sprang to his eyes and his hand flew to his brown leg where the man's staff had left a red velt.

I winced as if I'd been the one struck. "What is wrong with you? He's a child!"

The man turned to face me, and recognition made my stomach sour. Dr. Harrison had been a close acquaintance of my father's—one I'd always been happy to see leaving. Especially after I'd walked in on a discussion about the "hotbed of vice and disease" they'd called Pendle Street. They'd both made it clear that they viewed the lower classes as outcasts from all of England, drawn to the docks of Fairshaw by their greed. *If they only knew whose greed really ruled the world.*

In front of me, the man cleared his throat. "I was accosted by these gutter rats, and don't let them tell you otherwise, Miss Fairshaw."

I bit my tongue, wishing I could lambast him like I had Mr. Holloway, but I couldn't underestimate this man. "I don't care what they were doing. There's no reason to hit a child!"

He shook his head and gave a snort. "I'd hope your father had instilled a better sense of decorum in you. But perhaps your grief has made you forget the demands of your station? You must mourn him very much." His sympathetic expression didn't match the calculating gleam shining in his dark eyes.

I'd overheard enough gossip in the kitchens to know this abuse of the poor wasn't out of character for him. I swallowed, inwardly wincing at the way his eyes followed the movement of my throat. "Thank you for your concern, Dr. Harrison, but I am well. Now please let me see to the boy."

I stepped around him, but found the alleyway empty. Where had they gone? Did the little boy have anyone to look after his injury? My heart squeezed painfully in my chest.

"They ran off, of course. Trash." Vehemence dripped from his words, and he wrinkled his nose, as if the foul stench in the air were the children's fault.

Elizabeth stepped forward. "Let's return home, M'lady." She curtsied in the direction of the doctor. "Good day, Dr. Harrison." Then she gripped my elbow and pulled us out of the alley. I winced as pain traveled up my arm, but she marched on. Once we were out of earshot, she let me go and turned to face me with fire in her gaze. "Adelaide Fairshaw! I cannot believe you would try to face off with Dr. Harrison of all people. He's a big bully, and you know it!"

I wrung my gloved hands. "I had to do *something*. He would have hurt them!"

"I'm trying to keep you safe!" She blew out a breath, but her anger had faded by the time she spoke her next words. "I understand you want to help, but people like him believe they have gained their wealth by moral superiority, and nothing you say or do will ever change his mind." She turned the corner of the building and started towards home.

I caught up to her. "I wasn't trying to change his mind, Bets. Only distract him long enough to let the children escape."

She paused and turned. "You did do that, Adelaide. They got away, one with as little as a rap to the leg. They were lucky."

The probable truth of her words didn't make me feel any better. Knowing men like Dr. Harrison existed and seeing them in action were two different things. "I hate him. He's a vile, vicious man."

Elizabeth looped her arm through mine, and tugged. "I know. Let's go home and hate him over a nice cup of tea. What do you say?"

"Yes, please." I blew out a breath and let her pull me with her, just as the first drops of rain landed on the stiff crape of my dress.

Chapter 8

Frederick

I threw open the front door of the tiny apartment I called home and tossed my cap somewhere in the vicinity of the hook where it belonged. Another curse dropped. One in a long row of others as I'd made my way home. "I almost had it!"

Martha glanced over her shoulder from where she was seated at the table, pieces of fabric stacked up next to her. "Almost had what?"

"The *damned* Fairshaw Cat."

Her eyebrows rose. "You saw the Fairshaw Cat?"

"I was a hair's length away from touching it." The front of my body was slicked with mud from my dive after the fur ball that would change our lives once I got a hold of it.

Martha's eyes trailed from my neck to my toes. "Did you look for it in a mud puddle?"

I rolled my eyes. "How long until you're done working? It's late."

"As soon as I finish this stack of shirts." She nodded to the pile next to her. A wave of guilt hit as I stepped closer and noticed the dark shadows under her eyes. If I'd captured that cat, she could have stopped working herself to death.

I shrugged the muddy shirt over my head. My chest was filthy too. I couldn't very well go see Miss Fairshaw like this. I wasn't sure if she'd told me all she knew about the cat or not. Either way, it was in my best interest to woo her, and I'd been woefully unsuccessful so far. *Because she had another suitor?*

I thought back to earlier in the day when I'd spotted her in the arms of the blacksmith's son. Some street urchin had run across her path, knocking her off balance. She'd have eaten dirt if the man hadn't appeared out of thin air and grabbed her. I might have excused him for saving her, but he'd held onto her far longer than was proper. And then the way she'd gazed up at him, with a soft smile she'd never given me? That I wasn't going to forget so quickly.

I turned to my sister, far more on top of the Fairshaw gossip than I. "Is Nicholas Cromwell searching for the Fairshaw Cat?"

Martha's shoulders stiffened. She lowered her sewing, but didn't turn her head. "I don't think so. Why are you asking?"

"I saw him with Miss Fairshaw at the market. They seemed quite familiar with each other."

Martha let out what sounded like a choked laugh. "I don't think he's involved with her. He's a bachelor as far as the gossip goes."

She didn't meet my eyes, and suspicion tingled at the back of my neck. But why would she keep this from me? "You'd tell me if you knew?"

Finally, she turned, a light blush in her cheeks. "I would tell you, Frederick." She lowered her sewing to the table. "Did you hear that Dr. Harrison joined the search for the cat? Mary Collins said so, and she's usually quite reliable with her information."

I chewed on that piece of news for a moment. So his magic rocks were not his only attempt to find the cat. "You'd think he'd been given enough in life already."

Martha returned to her mending. "Men are always striving to better their stations, aren't they? I've yet to meet a man who has enough and is also content with his wealth."

"And when you do, you'll marry him?"

She bent her head low, inspecting what I knew to be a perfectly even row of stitches. "I sure will."

She'd told me this years ago, and I'd selfishly thanked fate she'd be unlikely to find such a man. But that had been before I understood the cruel life facing a woman born on Pendle Street. Now, I saw my sister in every drawn grimace I passed on the docks—in every aged beggar woman croaking out her prayers for a coin for bread. Would I spend fewer of my nights awake trying to find a way to better our circumstances if Martha got married? Under my care, her shoulders were already too hunched for a woman her age. The sharp bones of her jaw made it clear she didn't get near enough to eat. *I needed to find that cat.*

"Liv will be home tomorrow." Martha's voice cut through my miserable thoughts.

A spark of hope lit in my chest. "She will?"

"It's her day off for the month. I expect she'll be here in the afternoon."

I looked around the quiet room where a curly headed Liv had toddled around not so long ago. I missed her laughter between these bare walls. I missed the elaborate stories I'd had to make up to help her go back to sleep after a nightmare. "It's not the same without her here, is it? Do we have supper for her?"

"I saved the sausages. It's not much for each, but—"

"Let her have my portion. I'll figure something else out for myself." *Or I'd go without.* Liv deserved all the sausages, and she needed them more than I did. I glanced at the near empty pan of coal in the corner, and grabbed the bucket of water Martha kept in the kitchen. I could have heated the water, but not when it would compromise both my sisters' comfort tomorrow. These spring nights were still cool and every blanket we owned was worn thin from years of use. If dousing myself in icy water was what I had to do to make myself presentable to Miss Fairshaw *and* let my sisters sleep through the night without shivering, I would.

"I'm going to need you to refill that, Frederick." Martha's words hit the door as it closed behind me.

"Will do." I didn't even bother to crack the door, it was flimsy enough she'd hear me fine. I plunged my muddy shirt into the bucket, twisting it around until the mud stains were gone and my hands red from the cold water. Wringing it out the best I could, I draped it over a broken chair by the back door. I pulled in a quick breath and braced myself before pouring the remaining water over my head. A curse flew from my lips as goosebumps erupted all over my torso.

"Oh, keep quiet, Holloway, will you? You can give us a show another night. Some of us have babes that are sleeping." Mrs. Jones' voice sounded from across the fence. She might be ten years my senior, but she'd never gotten to the age where she understood privacy between neighbors. I didn't think her babies slept much as it was with her sharp voice cracking like a whip across the fence whenever something happened to catch her interest—and just about everything did. I rolled my eyes and tugged on my wet shirt. It slicked to my chest and didn't cover much more than it had on the chair.

Mrs. Jones gave a disappointed huff and slammed her backdoor on the way in. *So much for her sleeping children.*

CHAPTER 9

Adelaide

I pasted a smile onto my face as I greeted the scholars gathered in the hall of the Library. My father may not be here to meet with them, but the Fairshaw Library was still a center of knowledge, and the steady traffic of learned men had never let up in the ten days since his death. One man's gaze lingered too long on me, a smile tilting his mouth as I met his eyes. *Perhaps the motive of their visits had changed for some.*

Averting my gaze, I let it rest on a point over their heads and spoke as if the undue attention didn't bother me. "Stonier will show you to the east wing, where you should find what you need."

The crowd followed the old butler, and I let out a sigh of relief. I needed to see the housekeeper next. I'd let the cook know about the delivery of rhubarb as soon as we'd made it home yesterday, but would she agree that the fruit was fresh enough for the tarts I'd planned? I strode off to the kitchen, ignoring the sudden hush of whispers as I entered, and got to work. My duties kept me too busy to worry about the hunt for the Fairshaw Cat for the rest of the daylight hours. But as male servants replaced newly glowing oil lamps into the wall sconces, I lost the battle against my mind.

I returned to my room through golden hallways of flickering light—the reality of my situation sinking as heavy and dark over my shoulders as the night had over Fairshaw. I crawled through my window and onto the hop vine under a velvet sky devoid of stars. *I hoped he wouldn't bother me tonight.* But wait, were those footsteps I heard far below me?

I stilled, but the only sound was the breeze rustling the hop leaves. I let out a breath of relief. Why had it seemed so easy to ignore my last minutes of freedom ticking away until Mr. Holloway had joined the hunt? My groan crushed the quiet night. Wasn't it punishment enough that I had to listen to his unwavering belief that he'd catch the cat during his visits? Must he occupy my thoughts now, too?

I slipped back through the window, much later than usual, and with my thoughts no less muddled than before. Normally, my mind sorted itself easily in the fresh air, but his disturbing entry into my life had put a stopper to that.

Inside my bedchamber, with the window locked and shuttered, I settled at my writing desk. I dipped my fountain pen into ink as dark as my thoughts and paused it over the paper. A drop of darkness splattered from the steel point onto the white surface. I watched it spread out like a dark pool, and still no words came.

Mr. Holloway's speech wasn't riddled with slang, nor was he unkempt. Had I been wrong to question his honor? Or had the man raised on the wharves left me unharmed in a ploy to find the whereabouts of the cat? When he found out that I knew no such secrets, would he lose interest? Or only lose interest in my mind? Unease slithered down my spine.

His smile might be the kind that turned women of any age to putty, but in so many of my books the handsomest men were the cruelest. Charming rogues lacked honor the most, and the women in their lives allowed it—every trespass forgiven based on nothing but attractive features and disarming smiles.

Another thought struck. Mr. Holloway was the only of my suitors I'd met, but that didn't mean there weren't others worse than him. What if he'd meant his offer of friendship, and I'd truly offended him by declining? Goosebumps erupted across my chest and arms. Would he find the cat, marry me, and then punish me for my harsh words? *Only if he'd been a dishonorable man in the first place.*

I closed my eyes. I knew this, but knowing something in your mind and risking your happiness to see it come true were different things. Hardship brought out the best in humans, yet they strove to avoid it. If the hardship of a husband like Mr. Holloway made me a strong and pious woman, I still wouldn't welcome it.

A soft knock startled me out of my thoughts. I replaced the pen, and moved to the door. "M'lady?" The whisper that sounded through the wood was softer than Elizabeth's.

I cracked the door and found a small, pale face lit by the flickering light from a candle. "Livvie?"

The little housemaid that followed Elizabeth around in her daily tasks, stared up at me, a faint blush across her cheeks. "I heard pacing, and wanted to be certain you were all right, M'lady."

I smiled. "I'm all right, Livvie. Why are you up so late?"

Her eyes widened and she shrugged. "I couldn't sleep, M'lady, and...Miss Elizabeth snores." She murmured the last part, as if fearing a backlash.

I bit my lip to keep back my laugh. Elizabeth's snores had woken me from many a sound sleep. "She does snore, doesn't she?" I winked at the girl, pleased to draw a quick smile to her serious face.

"Why don't you come in here? We can talk for a bit if

you'd like, but there's also a cot at the end of my bed that Elizabeth sometimes uses, if you want to catch some sleep before morning. I don't think I snore, though I can't say for certain." In reality, my four poster bed had more than enough room for the girls Elizabeth and I had been, and the cot had only ever served to keep up appearances for my father's sake.

Livvie's dark eyes widened. "I couldn't do that, M'lady!"

"Of course you could. I invited you."

She hesitated. "But, M'lady, it wouldn't be proper, surely!"

I gripped her wrist gently and tugged. "Come, Livvie, the floorboards in the hallway must be freezing." I'd felt the draft as I'd opened my door.

Her eyes widened as she looked from my hand around her wrist to a spot over her shoulder. "But M'lady, Mrs. Tabor wouldn't like it, and—"

"And I will personally make sure she knows it was my idea." I understood her hesitation. Mrs. Tabor had put the fear of God in me a time or two when I'd been Livvie's age.

Hope shone in her eyes as she looked up at me. "You will?"

I nodded. "I promise."

Her face lit up. "Oh. Thank you, M'lady. It really is quite cold out here." She puffed out her candle and this time when I tugged at her hand, she entered my room.

I crossed the floor to sit on my bed and patted the space beside me. "Tell me a little bit about yourself. I'm sure you know all about me, and I know hardly anything about you."

Her tiny frame hardly moved the mattress as she sank onto it. She pulled in a breath, and stared at her hands. "My mother died ten years ago, when I was born. I grew up on Pendle Street, where Martha Holloway took care of me until I began to serve here, M'lady."

My ears perked at the name of Livvie's caretaker. "Is this Martha any relation to Mr. *Frederick* Holloway?"

She nodded eagerly. "His sister, M'lady."

My heart beat faster. I shouldn't pry. I didn't want to take advantage of Livvie, but I couldn't pass up a chance to learn more about the man that occupied so many of my thoughts. "Do you know Mr. Holloway well?"

The first big grin I'd seen from her stretched across her face. "Oh yes. I know him quite a lot, M'lady!"

"Will you tell me about him?"

She nodded, the mattress bouncing with her excitement. "Is it true like Miss Elizabeth says, he's in the lead to be your husband?"

It was an absurd statement, but also true. "So I've heard."

"I'm sure he would make a terrific husband, M'lady. He's very handsome and he's a kind brother to Martha and me."

"He considers you his sister?"

She grinned. "He says I'm his prettiest sister and Martha his smartest, M'lady."

I laughed at the importance in her voice. I'd known nothing about Mr. Holloway's family. That it counted more than blood relatives surprised me. "I haven't heard much good about him, I confess."

Livvie shook her head, blonde curls bouncing as she tsked in a way so reminiscent of Elizabeth, I held back another laugh. "That's only because the gossips are jealous of his success, M'lady. He brings Martha coins when she's out of bread, and lifts me way up in the air and swings me around when I see him, though Martha scolds him, because she says he ought to treat me like a lady, not a child." Her eyes sparkled and her scrawny chest puffed out her nightgown with pride.

Clearly, the man I wanted to hate was her very favorite. "You don't seem to mind?"

"I want to be treated like a lady, of course, but he is so strong, and I love to feel the air against my face as he spins me. He really is a very good man, M'lady." I tried to picture the scoundrel I'd come to know as a man who picked up his little sister and swung her around until she was out of breath with laughter, but couldn't.

Livvie yawned. "I better find my bed, M'lady." She grimaced. "Miss Elizabeth will wake me at dawn to polish the silver again, and it's not so far away."

"The offer for the cot still stands." Livvie's little forehead wrinkled. She tucked a blonde curl behind her ear as an intense debate showed clearly on her expressive face. The shadows under her eyes told me an uninterrupted night would do her wonders. "It's freshly made up, as I'm sure you know."

She fell asleep the second her head met the pillow. I stood at the end of the little pull-out cot and watched her sleep. Her blonde curls spread across her pillow, and dark lashes feathered her pale cheeks. She scrunched up her little face, then relaxed. Tucked under the comforter, she looked younger than her ten years.

Would it be like this to be a mother? I'd always wanted children, just not forced upon me by an arranged marriage. I touched my flat middle. Regardless of my feelings, I'd likely be a mother soon. *Hopefully the child won't be Mr. Holloway's.*

Or would that be so bad? His reputation gave him no

credit, but this little girl did. Which should I trust more? Livvie might be a child, but children didn't stay innocent long on the docks. Could she be right about her adoptive brother despite her tender age?

I undressed while my thoughts churned. Outside my window the dark hue of night had shifted to a lighter blue. Not quite dawn nor quite night. I hoped Livvie would get to sleep in as much as I would. I pulled the covers over myself. Elizabeth would rise in a few hours to light the fire in my room. I had no doubt my soft-hearted maid would take pity on the little girl asleep at my feet. I closed my eyes. *Yes, I was certain she'd leave us both to get our much needed rest.*

CHAPTER 10

Frederick

Miss Fairshaw was asleep. It had to be noon, and still she laid in her bed—with her window ajar. It seemed improbable that a magical library would rely on things like locks and closed windows to keep uninvited guests out, but no prickling sensation came as I touched the wooden sill. I ran my hand down the window pane and felt none of the pulsing magic from my first visit.

I shouldn't slip my finger past the sill and pull the window open—an honorable man wouldn't have. But as the gap between the glass and frame widened, I wasn't entirely sure that description fit me. I curled my fingers around the inside frame, still no tingling. No sign of a spell to keep me out. Irritation grated. *What if a hardened criminal sought entry into her bedchamber?* Why would she guard herself so poorly? She couldn't choose her groom, to be sure, but to be this flippant with her life and virtue? It didn't align with the spitfire I'd come to know.

I lifted my gaze, half expecting her fiery blue eyes to be staring back at me from the bed. Instead, pale lashes rested on skin that glowed in the warm sunlight. Were the shadows under her eyes from her late night visits to the hop branch above her window? Why hadn't I talked myself out of calling again this morning? It was a fool's errand. I'd offered my friendship three nights ago, and she'd sneered in my face. She and I weren't destined to be friends.

Her chest rose and fell as I tried to justify my presence in her bedchamber. *She might be my only clue to finding the cat.* If she wasn't, it made me no less certain I had what it would take to catch it. And when that happened, I had no desire to marry a woman who despised me.

I'd hoped a daylight visit would make her feel less on edge, aiding me in repairing our relationship. But I hadn't counted on finding her asleep. I pushed the window fully open and hoisted myself over the edge. No lighting struck me down as the soles of my boots landed on the polished wood floor.

I was inside the Fairshaw Library. Bubbling elation rose in my chest, and my blood pounded in my veins. I felt drunk with triumph and power as I took another step into the room. One more, and my frame shadowed her face from the sunlight. She shifted, furrowed her brow, and stretched her arms above her head. The covers slipped lower to reveal the frilly nightgown covering her chest. I swallowed and shifted my gaze to her face.

As if sensing my presence, her eyes opened. A moment's confusion gave way to terror—then anger. I'd never even heard the curse she used, but it should have made any highborn lady blush. *Not her.* I grinned. "Good morning, Miss Fairshaw."

She sat upright, clasping the covers up under her chin. "What are you doing in my room?"

I shrugged. "The window was open."

"And that gave you leave to enter?"

I straightened. "With all the Fairshaw's magic, I expected a spell to keep strangers out."

Her eyes widened. "There is one!" Her gaze moved from me to the window and back again as her cheeks darkened. *Interesting.*

"Pray, what is the spell, Miss Fairshaw?"

She pressed her lips together. "I'm afraid it's none of your concern, Sir." I narrowed my eyes. What was she hiding? She straightened as her gaze flew to the foot of the bed and worry stole into her expression. "You shouldn't be here. Do you have any idea what this will look like?"

"It's news to me that we have an audience, Miss Fairshaw."

"We don't." Her gaze settled back on me, but the unease stayed in her eyes.

A rustle sounded, and I frowned, turning to look closer at the spot where her eyes had lingered. "What are you not telling—"

"Frederick!" Liv's jubilant voice was the last thing I'd expected to hear in Miss Fairshaw's sunny bedchamber. My little sister jumped up from beyond the foot of the bed, rumpled curls surrounding her sleepy face.

I frowned. "What are you doing here, Liv?"

"What are *you* doing here, in M'lady's bedchamber—" She slapped a tiny hand to her mouth. "I'm so sorry, M'lady!" Her wide eyes were glued to the face of the woman in the bed. "I meant no disrespect, I promise!" Protectiveness bristled in me at the horror on Liv's face, but I saw nothing on Miss Fairshaw's face that warranted the fear in my sister's voice.

"It's fine, Livvie." Her words held no reproach. "Though please don't tell anyone of this."

"Not Miss Elizabeth, either, M'lady?"

Miss Fairshaw shook her head sternly. "No, please don't tell Miss Elizabeth."

"I won't, M'lady, I promise." Liv clasped her hands together as if making a vow. She glanced at me, then at her mistress. "May I speak to Mr. Holloway, please, M'lady?"

Miss Fairshaw's head dipped, and Liv threw herself into my arms.

"Hi Liv." A real smile stretched across my face for the first time this morning. Her slight weight in my arms felt more solid than I remembered. And as much as it shamed me *I* hadn't provided it for her, my soul settled a little deeper at the thought that she had enough to eat. *Finally.*

Liv's dark eyes lit with anticipation. "You're going to swing me, right?"

"In here? This isn't Pendle Street." The disappointment on her face slayed me. I blew out a breath. "Okay, then." Ignoring Miss Fairshaw's raised eyebrows, I twirled my sister until her breathless laughter filled the room. I lowered her to a stand and held onto her scrawny arm as she staggered from side to side while her dizziness subsided. "Now, may I speak to your mistress in private?"

"Of course." She giggled, a light sound that never failed to make my heart jolt with pleasure. Then, as if remembering herself, her eyes lifted to her mistress who was discreetly shaking her head.

I turned towards the head of the bed. "Miss Fairshaw, if I may have a word."

Fire blazed in her eyes for a split second, but it disappeared as she turned to Liv. "You may go, Livvie. But not a word about this, please."

"You have my word, M'lady." She curtsied, and walked to open a door hidden almost entirely by wallpaper. She shut the door quietly behind herself, and we were alone.

I turned to the woman who now made no show of hiding the anger on her face. "How dare you enter my bedchamber while I'm asleep?"

I chuckled. "To be fair, I didn't expect you to be. It's almost midday."

"I can't believe you'd be brazen enough to waltz in here, and—"

Was she serious? "I can't believe I'd be *able* to. Why was the window ajar? Why was I able to enter through the spell?"

She flushed. "My housemaid must have opened the window this morning. It was shut when I went to bed."

"And the spell I circumvented?" I stepped closer, and she squared her shoulders, a haughty look slipping into her eyes.

"Why would I tell you the secrets of the Library?"

"Because the blush on your face makes me think it has something to do with me."

Her eyes shot daggers. Then she looked to the door where my sister had disappeared. "How do you know Livvie?"

"She's my sister."

She raised an eyebrow. "By blood?"

I narrowed my eyes at her. "Since when does blood matter? She's my sister as much as the one borne by my mother."

"She says you're good to her." Her words were quiet, as if they weren't meant for my benefit. A small spark of triumph lit in my chest. If she'd asked Liv about me, perhaps all was not lost?

I couldn't help the satisfied smirk that crossed my face. "Now why would you ask my sister about me, Miss Fairshaw?"

She shrugged as the pink color deepened in her cheeks. "I wanted to make sure you were good to her."

My eyebrows rose. "She told you I wasn't the villain you accused me of being?"

She shifted uncomfortably. "I didn't—"

"You did accuse me of that. And you refused to believe I didn't intend to harm you."

She made a move as if to get up, but abruptly stopped and pulled the covers tighter around her body. "You're trying to further dissuade me of that opinion by sneaking into my bedchamber while I'm asleep?"

I snorted. "I came in the window because I wanted to talk to you, nothing else."

Her nostrils flared. "You were standing over my bed!"

That did make me look bad. I rubbed a hand across my face. "I did nothing but watch you sleep."

"Does not make you sound any better! Would you have done more if Livvie hadn't been here?"

Infuriating woman! "Of course not!"

She sniffed. "You're not making it easy to believe you."

I nodded towards the window. "Why don't you come out to the hop vine, Miss Fairshaw, and we can talk in a more proper setting?"

"I need a few minutes to get dressed."

Humor tugged my lips. "I'd gladly talk to you as you are. Though perhaps not in public." She rolled her eyes and tilted her head towards my exit in a clear dismissal. But as I crossed the floor and crawled out through the window, I was certain I'd glimpsed a tug at the corner of her full mouth.

CHAPTER 11

Frederick

The clocktower chimed one as Miss Fairshaw climbed out the window. In the daylight her perch so close to the top of the Fairshaw Library seemed even more precarious than it had at night. I reached my hand out, and with the smallest bit of hesitation, she gripped it and pulled herself up to the vine where I sat.

The sunlight caught her blonde hair, turning it again to the spun gold I remembered from our first meeting. But the tilt of her lips, that had been nowhere then, now spiked my pulse. "And for what pressing matter did you feel the need to disturb my sleep, Mr. Holloway?"

A grin tugged at my mouth. I lowered my voice and spoke with an air of confidentiality. "I wasn't aware anyone but badgers and drunkards slept during the daytime, Miss Fairshaw, and you didn't strike me as either."

"Quite the astute observation, Mr. Holloway." Her lips twitched. A small victory, but I'd get a laugh out of her yet.

A bird rustled through the cluster of leaves by her head and took flight. Miss Fairshaw startled forward. The movement tipped her off balance, and her arms flailed. Her panicked scream filled my ears.

My arm shot out and crashed against her body. Pain shot through my shoulder. For a moment that felt like an eternity, all I could hear was the blood roaring in my ears.

She gasped for breath, her nails dug painfully into my arm, clutching it with strength I didn't know she possessed. Her face was ghastly white. What would I do if she fainted out here on the vine? *Please don't faint.* I moved closer. "Are you…all right?"

Blue eyes, full of disbelief, met mine. "You saved me."

I rolled my eyes. Had she thought I'd let her die without lifting a finger? Then my imagination filled in the horrible details of this moment had I moved any slower, or worse, if she'd been alone. Anger heated my blood and laced my voice. "Please tell me this has never happened before, Adelaide."

She shuddered and her throat worked. "I promise nothing like this has ever happened."

"Good." *So help me God, if it ever happened again, I would lock her up.* Except, I had no such authority in her life. Not yet.

Adelaide's gaze fell on the sleeve of my coat where her

nails still attempted to dig through the fabric. She loosened her grip, and her trembling hand ran over the indentations on my sleeve. "I'm so sorry, Mr. Holloway. I shouldn't have…" Her words trailed off.

Shouldn't have what? Was it not considered proper for a lady to attempt to save herself from a fall to her death?

"A clawed arm seems a small price to pay not to get charged with your murder, Miss Fairshaw." I removed my coat, and pushed my shirtsleeve up to reveal the faint bruises from her nails. They'd heal. The years she'd shaved off my life by her brush with death, I wasn't so sure about.

Her brows drew together. "I can't believe you can joke about this."

"I'm not joking, Miss Fairshaw. What do you think would have happened, if you'd tumbled to your death, and the beaks found me climbing down towards your body? They wouldn't think any more highly of me than you do."

"Maybe they'd be wrong."

Her voice was so quiet I thought I'd misheard her. Hope flared in my chest, and I leaned closer. "You no longer think me a villain?"

Her fists clenched in her skirts as she looked out over the bustling town beneath us. "It's difficult to view anyone searching for the Fairshaw Cat as anything but."

Her words surprised me. Edward Fairshaw's disdain for the lower classes had been well-known. Did his daughter feel the same way? The little boy who'd told me wide-eyed about the proper lady who'd saved him and his sister from a violent toff hadn't given me that impression. His story had made it sound like her temper wasn't confined to any social standing. But why was searching for the cat so firmly on her list of sins? "You don't want it to be found?"

Her throat worked. "Since the day I killed my mother, my father had no interest in me or my fate. He left me at my mother's deathbed without regard for my well-being. I think ever since, whenever he looked at me, he saw nothing but my mother's life seeping out of her." The lack of emotion in her voice tore at me. "Since Fairshaw marriages are lifelong and can't be dissolved, whoever marries me will be tied to me for the rest of my days. I don't want another absent man to limit my life like my father did, nor do I want a man who only wants to control me."

"Are those your only options?"

She shrugged, but her lips pressed together as if words she didn't want to share would well out if she didn't keep them closed.

No wonder she fought against the idea of marriage. I'd always thought I'd envy Miss Fairshaw's charmed upbringing. Now I wondered if I hadn't had the better part.

Despite the hunger pains at night and the scars from work no child should do, I could still feel my mother's gentle touch against my cheek after a bad dream. Even after her death, I'd slept in Martha's scrawny arms for days as a fever raged through my body, after a broken pulley had sent a crate barreling into my shoulder. Had Adelaide had *anyone* to mother her like that?

She sat with her back straight and her head held high, looking every bit the haughty lady I'd assumed her. Looking closer, her face was still pale, and her throat worked. Had I judged her too harshly? What must her life have been like without a mother or siblings, and her only blood relative a father who ignored her? And I'd barged into her world and asked her to help me be the next person to rule her life. Compassion tugged at my heart.

"I'd like to prove you wrong, Miss Fairshaw. There are men who do not control or neglect, even if your father wasn't among them." She didn't answer, but her shoulders straightened the tiniest bit.

Chapter 12

Adelaide

I crept through town in the early morning light, careful not to slip on cobblestones still wet from last night's rain. The sun had barely risen, and over the lake fairies could be seen dancing in the mist. *Or so my nurse had told me long ago.* Mist or fairies, I caught glimpses of the gauzy, white haze between the houses as I ventured farther away from the safety of the Fairshaw Library.

Escaping without Elizabeth noticing had been a challenge, and the housekeeper would be scandalized if she found out I'd ventured outside without a chaperone. Much more if she'd known where I was headed. But I didn't want anyone to accompany me on this errand.

I hitched up my dark skirts. The movement jostled the basket of sweetbreads I'd nabbed as the cook had turned to order a scullery maid to mop up a spill. Whether the pastries would be a peace offering or a bribe, I didn't know.

I slowed my gait as I neared the docks. What if I'd miscalculated the time? He'd be upset with me if he knew my errand, and I'd die of embarrassment if he caught me red-handed.

But I didn't want to be fooled by Mr. Holloway's charming smile or the mischievous sparkle in his eyes. I had the wisdom of the Fairshaw Library on my side, I just needed more information. And I knew just how to get it. I raised my hand and my knuckles made contact with the weather worn door.

The low timbre of a man's voice from the other side of the door turned my stomach to ice. *He couldn't be here!* I'd purposely gone at a time when I was certain he wouldn't be around. A door closed softly somewhere beyond the threshold, then light steps approached. The door creaked open and a woman around my own age peeked out. Her face paled as recognition dawned. "Miss Fairshaw? Has anything befallen my sister?"

"I'm not here about Livvie, Miss Holloway. May I come in?" Better to be out of the street and hidden from view sooner rather than later.

Her breath of relief was audible, and she shot a quick glance over her shoulder before the door opened wide enough for me to step across the threshold. "Certainly, M'lady."

Mr. Holloway's childhood home was as cramped as Livvie had described it, but also surprisingly attractive. The sparse room was tidy and the dirt floor swept. Three spindly chairs stood around a table that had seen better days. But the tabletop was clean, and the glass chimney of a small lamp sparkled in the light from the fireplace.

I held out my offering of sweetbreads, and a genuine smile spread on Miss Holloway's face. "Please have a seat. May I offer you some tea, Miss Fairshaw?" She turned towards the fireplace, poked the coals until they glowed and slid a kettle over the heat.

I flexed my fingers to keep them from twisting in the fabric of my skirts as Miss Holloway prepared my tea. *I just needed her to tell me whether or not her brother could be trusted—then I could leave.* Finally, she placed a chipped cup of the steaming brew in front of me. The thin milk she poured in barely lightened the color. She replaced the kettle, pulled a rickety chair out from the other side of the table, and sat.

"My question is about your brother, Miss Holloway." Surprise lit her features and again she glanced toward the backdoor. I cleared my throat. "He's not here, is he?"

She shook her head. "I haven't seen him since last night, M'lady." Then why was her attention on the door at the back of the room? Had my ears played tricks on me when I'd heard the rumble of a male voice? Was Mr. Holloway even now leaning against the other side of that door, listening to our conversation?

"If you have questions about his progress in the cat hunt, I'm afraid I can't tell you much. The walls in this part of town have ears. Especially anything that can earn the eavesdropper coins, as news about the Fairshaw Cat surely would." Miss Holloway lowered her teacup. "My brother sought you out to try to find the cat, didn't he? And *not* in a proper way?"

My cheeks heated. "He climbed my wall, and came upon me undressing for a bath." Too late, I remembered the thin walls. Was that a muffled snort from the vicinity of the backdoor? I rose from my seat, my gaze intent on the slab of wood concealing the offender. "Is someone here?"

"A friend. Not one who would spill your secrets, I assure you, M'lady."

I returned my gaze to Miss Holloway's pink cheeks, and understanding dawned. "Is that because I now know a secret of his?" Her entertaining a male visitor barely past dawn would be quite the scandal. But perhaps she wouldn't stay unmarried long.

"Please don't think anything untoward of me or my family. It's not a secret so much as two people trying to avoid wagging tongues."

Feeling bolder, I lowered to my chair. "That is the reason for my visit, actually. Your brother's reputation does him no favors."

"But?"

I pushed out a breath of frustration. "But, then he apologized for his words, and Livvie talks of him as if he's the rising sun she adores. Seeing them together makes me think a sister couldn't be loved better. I can't tell which he is—the honorable brother, or the wicked opportunist."

"Could he not be both?" Her dark eyes met mine. "My brother has not always made honorable choices. I'm sure you know enough of his upbringing to fill in what you don't. He wasn't much older than Livvie is now when our mother died, and after that he was far more reckless than he'd ever been before. I tried my best to keep him out of trouble, but there is only so much an older sister can do. Especially one still a child herself."

"I didn't intend to blame you—"

"I didn't think you did, Miss Fairshaw. My brother's mistakes are his own to bear."

But the story of his mother's death didn't answer the question circling my mind. "Can I trust him?"

"That's not something I can tell you." I tried to keep the disappointment from my expression, but Miss Holloway must read emotions as well as her brother. "I'm sorry I can't give my brother a ringing endorsement. I will say, he always acts with honor towards those he loves."

I left the Holloways' cramped apartment with an empty basket and no more answers than I'd come there with. As I walked home, bleary-eyed women with knit shawls wrapped tightly around their too-thin bodies hurried through the streets. Children younger than Livvie, in trousers that barely hit below their knees and shirts that looked more like rags, stood at the street corners. Ready to run errands for a coin.

I kept my head low. I didn't think anyone would be so desperate as to attack me in the middle of the street during daytime hours, but I couldn't be sure. An air of desperation hung over the city, and desperate men were always dangerous.

I turned down a path through the Fairshaw woods. The twitter of birds was a hundred times better than the gossip that had surrounded me on market day and surely would do so if I walked back through town. The sun warmed my shoulders as I pondered Miss Holloway's words.

Her brother might treat those he loved with kindness and honor, and he *had* saved my life. But he didn't *love* me, and I was certain love wasn't what he wanted from finding the Fairshaw Cat. In the end, his two sisters might very well hold all the affection he was able to give.

CHAPTER 13

Adelaide

Lost in illusions of freedom, I'd watched the fiery color of the sunset give way to the dimness of night. The fresh air of early spring cool against my cheeks, my hands resting on the solid bark, and the town of Fairshaw spread out beneath me. There was no need here to worry about the scullery maid who'd been let go for stealing silverware. Or the scholar who'd cornered me in the west wing this morning, before Stonier had come to my rescue. On this vine I needn't make decisions or rule over people who met my reasonable questions with scorn.

Long after night fell over the world, a shadowed figure slid onto the hop vine. A burst of fear ignited in my chest. Blood pounded in my ears, and breath refused to enter my lungs. Had another man discovered my secret? One who, unlike Mr. Holloway, wouldn't leave without a conclusive answer to the whereabouts of the Fairshaw Cat?

But this man's movements seemed familiar, and sudden

moonlight over the planes of his handsome face made me certain. My shoulders sagged, and I pulled in a full breath. "You startled me."

I expected him to apologize, but he frowned, and his voice held as much chiding as mine had. "You didn't notice me climbing up the vine? I should hope you'd be a little more alert when sitting out here unprotected in the dark!"

I ignored the disgust in his voice as well as the thrill in my chest at this glimmer of protectiveness. *Or was it only protectiveness for property that might soon be his?* Had his quick response yesterday been the same?

My heart sank.

"What use is a spell that protects the Library when you can freely leave whenever you please?"

What did he know about the spells encasing the Library? They weren't common knowledge. I didn't think even my father had known half of them. I narrowed my eyes. "I have no need to defend the Fairshaw Library's inner workings, least of all to you. But yes, I can leave whenever I please. At least until the Fairshaw Cat is found."

And the more I thought about that moment, the more I thought that I might just want to leave before it ever got that far. I could run away, couldn't I? Or were there spells in place to keep me from escaping the town of Fairshaw, too? I'd never left Fairshaw lands, so I truly didn't know.

"You'll be locked in here when the key is found?"

I shrugged and tried to give off the air of nonchalance I so desperately desired. "And busy getting into my wedding gown."

Mr. Holloway turned toward me, dark eyes narrow as they measured me in the half light. "You have a wedding dress already?" His voice dripped with accusation, but how could he be shocked at this?

I'd glimpsed the gown in the dressmaker's room this morning on my way back from his sister's. The fabric had looked just like the hazy morning mist over Fairshaw Lake, the lace like softly spun cobwebs, and the gemstones had captured the glittering sunlight in all its glory. It was without a doubt the most beautiful garment I'd ever laid eyes on. But it brought me no joy. Flatness stole into my voice. "Of course I have a wedding gown, Mr. Holloway. My wedding is imminent, after all. We're only waiting for the groom."

"Me."

I rolled my eyes. Did his cockiness know any limits? "You can't know that any more than I can. It could be anyone." I wrapped my arms around myself as if the warmth could save me from my fate.

"I know I usually achieve that which I put my mind

to." In the moonlight, his dark eyes gleamed—hungry for the power he thought would be his. But magic couldn't be bought—a secret both Mr. Holloway and the rest of the desperate men trailing woods and moors around town calling for the Fairshaw Cat would soon know. Any man might use his courage and cunning to find the key, win the great Fairshaw Library and my hand in marriage. But the Fairshaw magic itself had to be earned—like my heart.

The moon slipped behind a cloud, leaving us in darkness. *What if my heart was so easily won I fell in love with Mr. Holloway?* I already sat outside, comfortably talking to him in the dark. How much longer until my accelerated heartbeat made me forget about the greed in his eyes when he spoke of the cat hunt?

It scared me now, but what if love made me see past it? I thought of the many intelligent women I'd read about, who'd loved men nothing short of devils. Would I love this man if he turned out to be a monster? *Oh please, let me not be so easily fooled.*

"Liv told me about the spell." The timbre of Frederick's voice brought me out of my dark thoughts and into the black night next to him. I knew which darkness I preferred. *Were my efforts not to fall for him already a lost cause?*

"She told me it's impossible to enter the Fairshaw Library unless one is wanted there by a Fairshaw." I felt his expectant gaze on me. "Which means you wanted me to enter your Library, your bedchamber." Moonlight lit on his victorious smirk, and mortification burned in my cheeks.

I'd always assumed the Library magic judged the mind of the Fairshaw, but what if it didn't? *And if the magic truly discerned the heart, how much worse the consequences of loving a man whose ambitions were greed and power?*

"You have nothing to say? Not even one of those colorful oaths, Miss Fairshaw?" His voice held nothing but triumph, and I wanted to hide from the knowing glint in his eyes. Hide, too, from the fate that seemed nothing but a net closing around me, cutting me off from all but this purpose I didn't want.

I wanted to retreat to the safety of my bedchamber. Unfortunately, Frederick sat like a barrier between me and my freedom. "What is there to say, Mr. Holloway?"

His deep chuckle colored the night air and warmed my insides. "I don't know, Miss Fairshaw, you could admit you like me?"

Refusing to crumble under the embarrassment, I clutched the cold bark of the vine and willed my hands not to shake. "That's taking it too far, Mr. Holloway, don't you think?"

His chest puffed out. "I don't." *He wouldn't.* Aggravating, cocky man he was.

"I believe you enjoy my company, Miss Fairshaw." His voice was the sing-songy one used by school boys teasing their classmates. "I wonder what else you'd like." I had no time to decipher that statement before his hand closed over mine. White hot tingles exploded over every inch of skin his warm palm covered. It felt exactly like the sparkling tension of magic. *But it wasn't.*

"What are you doing?" I forced my voice to sound as scandalized as it ought to. It was bad enough that we'd formed a habit of spending time together alone, unchaperoned, in the dark—I absolutely couldn't allow him to touch me!

Frederick's fingers curled around mine. The skitters of tension that prickled across my skin, the heat spreading in my chest—it spelled trouble, all of it. "You can't do this! I mean, *I* can't—"

He made a sound as if to shush a fussy infant. "I'm only holding your hand, Miss Fairshaw." His overbearing tone made me want to pull my hand away. *I was right about this!* He shouldn't act like our relationship was a settled matter when that was the furthest thing from the truth. Any man in this town could claim me as his bride at any given moment, and the rapid beat of my pulse and the flutter in my belly were the last things I needed.

"I know you think you'll find the cat, but what if you don't?" I whispered the words as my pulse hammered in the palm of the hand I'd made no attempt to move.

"Then I'll have held your hand as a friend, Miss Fairshaw." He laced his fingers between mine. Flickers of magic shot up my arm again, and my stomach somersaulted in a way it never had the hundreds of times I'd held Elizabeth's hand.

My heart beat too erratically. I needed a distraction. "Have you seen anything of the cat?" He shrugged, as if hunting for this animal hadn't been his sole focus since my father's death. "How are you going to find it?"

He stiffened. "I'm not telling you that."

I wiggled my fingers, trying to wrestle them out of his. I couldn't. "Frederick. Let me go."

He released my hand, but as he straightened, his grin was triumphant. "Did you just call me by my given name?"

Mortification flared hot on my neck, and I wanted to melt through the vine into nothingness. When had I begun to think of him as Frederick rather than Mr. Holloway?

"I didn't think you'd be so easily flustered, Miss Fairshaw." His smirk was everything I wanted to hate about him.

"Don't get used to it."

"Oh, but I think I will." Mischief glinted in his eyes, and the air that had chilled me earlier suddenly didn't feel cool enough.

"Shouldn't you be off to find that cat?"

His smirk didn't fade like I'd expected. Instead, he leaned close, and his breath fanned my face. My heart slammed into my throat. If he got any closer, our noses would bump. Our mouths would—

His breath smelled faintly like apples. My pulse pounded. But then he paused his descent. Waiting for what? My permission?

His warm mouth pressed against my forehead. "Goodnight, Miss Fairshaw." He rose to his feet in one swift movement. My mouth dropped open as indignation and pleasure fought for space in my brain. My forehead tingled where he had *kissed me*. Frederick had dropped a kiss on my forehead as if he was… As if we—

He stood above me and took in my shocked expression with eyes that sparkled with mischief. "Are you confused at my formal address, Miss Fairshaw? It seemed prudent that one of us should keep up the propriety in this relationship."

I gasped. "That's not what you did!"

He dropped from the vine, and I leaned forward to keep him in sight. His voice rose up from several feet below me. "What was that, Miss Fairshaw?"

"That was *not* proper!"

"My apologies, Miss Fairshaw, I fear I'm too far down to hear you." Yards below me, he was barely a shadow in the sparse light. I wished I could climb fast enough to follow him down and give him a piece of my mind. Or better yet, shake some sense into him. He couldn't do this! My heart wasn't impervious to tenderness as his must be!

"Goodnight, love!" With a tip to his tophat, Frederick dropped from the last branch. His feet smacked the cobblestone, and I wanted to smack him just as firmly.

He sauntered away down the cobbled street and turned the corner as if he hadn't just upended my world. I touched my fingers to where his lips had been, dropped my face into my hands, and groaned. *I wasn't free to love in the first place, and no way was I going to fall in love with that man.* I pressed a hand to my thundering heart. Had the damage been done already?

CHAPTER 14

Frederick

Filtered through the leafy canopy above, sunlight dappled the meandering trail through the Fairshaw woods. My back and shoulders ached from watching that same path since early this morning. But while I'd spotted several birds, a pair of red squirrels, and a hare in all that time, nothing had caught my interest like the dark-clad figure striding through the woods now. Adelaide, without as much as a lady's maid to protect her. Did she not realize the risk she was taking?

I shifted on the damp log where I sat hidden from view by the leaves of several young saplings. On the trail, Adelaide halted. Her gaze searched for the source of movement, head tilted to catch the next rustle of leaves. I sat unmoving until she resumed her walk. Could she be here to meet a lover? I didn't like the idea, but it would explain why she denied her feelings for me. It had been clear last night that she wasn't as indifferent as she liked to pretend.

I flicked a leaf with my finger, and she stilled like a startled rabbit about to bolt. With a grin, I rendered the hours I'd spent in the woods useless, stood from the cover of leaves, and fought my way through the brush toward her. She surprised me by holding her ground until recognition flared on her face. "Frederick—Mr. Holloway."

Faint color appeared in her cheeks, and my grin widened. "Out for a stroll alone in the woods? That doesn't seem entirely safe for a person in your position, Miss Fairshaw."

Her brows lowered, drawing that angry spark I loved to her eyes. "And what position might that be?"

"That of a woman holding the secrets to the most wanted animal in Fairshaw." I stepped so close my shoulder brushed hers, and her soft intake of breath was music to my ears.

"You know I don't know anything about where the cat can be found."

That I believed her didn't make whatever errand she was on any safer. "I don't believe that is the common opinion. Who's to say someone hunting for the cat won't try to pry it out of you in much more unpleasant ways than I have?"

She retreated a step, and I rolled my eyes. Why did she always assume my words were veiled threats? "Not *me.*

What reason do I have to accost you in the woods? If that was my end goal, I'd have succeeded long ago."

She snorted, but held her distance. "I hope you don't think that makes you sound any better, Mr. Holloway."

I fought a smile. "Do you honestly think I want to harm you?"

She searched my eyes, and the fire in hers retreated. "No, I don't."

Thank God for that! I must be getting through to her a little. A rustle sounded from my hiding place in the bushes, and I grabbed her arm. "Let's go. You shouldn't stay so long in one spot, especially not one this secluded."

I pushed her ahead of me, but she dug her heels into the dirt. "Who invited you along for my walk?"

"I invited myself. Now, come on, before whoever is coming through the woods sees you and realizes his opportunity."

But the crash through the underbrush behind us told me we were too late. A slurred voice rang through the woods. "Ey! Is that Master Fairshaw's daughter?"

"It is, by golly! Hey little lady, we'd like to have a word with you." A second male voice accompanied the breaking of twigs behind us.

I glanced over my shoulder at the group emerging from the woods and groaned. Too many to take on if they wanted a fight, and judging by the shrill whistles and leering smiles, they definitely did.

"Here, kitty kitty!" The speaker's eyes roved over Adelaide's body, a confident smirk sliding onto his face. Probably much like the one I'd sported when we'd first met. Was this how she saw me?

The other men guffawed at the joke, and my gaze fell on Adelaide's fancy walking boots. "Can you run in those?"

"I'm not going to—" Her words ended on a squeak as I swept her up in my arms and started running.

"Hey! He's trying to take the kitty away from us!" The hammering of boots sounded behind us as the men gave chase.

Adelaide's sharp intake of breath was either fear or indignation, but whatever she saw over my shoulder made her cease her struggle to get down, easing my load considerably. Fear thinned her voice. "Frederick, they're catching up."

"I've got you." I wheezed the words against a lock of hair that had escaped the pins under her hat. I wasn't going to be able to keep this up long. Spotting a smaller trail ahead of us, I sprinted towards it.

"Put me down. I can run." I stumbled over a root and almost threw her on the ground, but she caught herself and followed the trail winding between the trees. She was right—she could run. Even if her boots would be wrecked with mud long before we found a way to safety.

A familiar rockwall up ahead made my heart jolt. I knew where we were—and better, where we could hide! "Adelaide, this way!"

If we could get inside the broken down walls of the old church, we'd be hidden completely from the trail. I pushed her gently toward the ruin I'd played in as a child. Years had passed since I'd last won a game of hide and seek between the dilapidated walls, but if I was lucky, the inner structures were still intact. I searched the outlines of rooms overgrown with herbs and young trees since I last played here. Finally I spotted the place I remembered, and my shoulders sank in relief. Could I find a way to convince the wealthiest woman in all of Fairshaw to crawl into the wine cellar behind the crumbled wall?

"Here, see that opening?" I pointed to the barely visible crevice between the mossy rocks.

"I see it." Without prodding, she closed the distance and squeezed through. In another moment she was hidden from view. Curses rang through the trees behind me as I followed her. My shoulders scraped painfully against the rough rock surface as I attempted to slip inside like Adelaide had, but my size did me no favors. The last time I'd used this hideout, I'd been at least a foot shorter and my shoulders nowhere near as broad. Ripping fabric sounded twice before I was finally hidden. It didn't matter—I could get a new coat when I was the Fairshaw Master.

Inside, I could easily stand up in the small room, but my shoulders brushed the wall on both sides of my body, and Adelaide's skirts seemed to fill whatever space was left. For several long minutes we held still as the shouted curses faded with the increasing distance between us and our pursuers.

"How do you know about this place?" Her whispered words cracked the tense quiet, and I turned to gaze at her over my shoulder. Her hat sat askew on her head, her cheeks bloomed with color, and her eyes seemed to sparkle from our run—and I'd never seen her look more beautiful.

I cleared my throat, still keeping my voice at a whisper. "I used to play here as a child."

She tugged off her black gloves and tucked them into her skirt pocket. Then she went to work getting her tilting hat all the way off, loosening the long pins as she went. "You used to be a child, Mr. Holloway?" The teasing in her low voice and the glint of mischief in her eyes made my heart thud a little faster.

I maneuvered my body in the small space until I could

face her fully. "Did you never play in these woods yourself? You're not that far from home."

She huffed. "My father scarcely let me out of the Library. I played with the children of servants, but only in secret. He didn't think my intellect would profit from the company of the lower classes."

Her quiet words were wistful, and sadness twisted in my chest. The Fairshaw gardens were famous for their fragrant herbs and rare flowers, the intricate pathways and hidden alcoves. Surely she'd spent many hours there. But could their cultivated, tamed beauty ever replace the wild allure of the woods to a child? My heart ached for the girl she'd once been. "If I become Fairshaw it won't be like that. Our children will get to play in the woods."

"If?" A smile played at the corners of her mouth. "It's the first I've heard you speak as if it was a question. You've seemed terribly sure of yourself so far."

"Like those men back in the clearing?" She pulled her lip between her teeth, and my heart sank. Did she really see me that way? "You can speak freely, Miss Fairshaw."

"I admit your approach seemed much like theirs when I met you."

"And now?" I held my breath as her eyes searched mine. Did she see a man like the ones we had just escaped? Willing to frighten, and even harm her, for their own

103

gain? Or did she see the man I wanted to be more for each day I spent with her? Her hesitation put a fire under me to show her my true colors. Before I'd made the decision to do so, I lifted my hand to her face and let my fingertips slide along her smooth, warm jaw. Need pulsed through my veins.

I wanted to kiss her.

I almost had last night, before I'd found a last thread of restraint and pressed my lips to her forehead instead. But this time the temptation might prove too much. I drew in a breath and leaned in.

"Frederick."

My whispered name was a warning I didn't want to heed. Not when the sweet scent of her breath pushed away the damp, earthy one of the mossy ruins surrounding us.

"Adelaide." The word was a strangled plea. Still she withdrew, and I missed the warmth of her body as she put as much space as possible between us.

"Do you think they're gone?" Her voice was breathy. Did she want me like I wanted her? Was her hesitation for the propriety of our situation only?

I cleared my throat, but my voice emerged a croak. "Who?"

"The men you rescued me from."

I held still and listened, but nothing. No movement

sounded from outside the ruin. "They're gone, I think."

She let out a breath. Of relief? "Let's go, then. This place won't do us any good."

That depended on who you asked—I wouldn't mind some more time with her here. I squeezed through the opening, and held out a hand for her. She slipped her fingers into mine and gingerly stepped out behind me. I paused again to listen, but only the gentle rustle of leaves in the breeze met my ears.

My eyes caught on Adelaide's small hand enclosed in mine. I longed to touch more of her, to reach out and smooth the wild tangle of hair left from our run. Instead, I brushed my thumb across her cheek, removing the smudge of dirt left there by our hiding place. Her breath caught, and my pulse sped up—

"Can I ask you something?" She spoke quickly, as if she needed to get the words out before her courage failed her.

"Anything." I desperately wanted her to trust me enough to speak freely. She bit her lip, and I quickly averted my eyes.

"Did you… When you helped me escape just now, did you do it to rescue *me*, or…to protect your interests?" The question hit like a bucket of water over my desire. Even after what had just happened, she still didn't trust my intentions? Had I read her so wrong?

I dropped her hand, and indifference slipped into my voice. "How are the two different?" Her hurt gasp stung worse than a slap across my face. A tear slid down her cheek, and I regretted my words immediately. "Adelaide, I didn't mean that."

"Please, Mr. Holloway. Don't worry about it. You've already made it quite clear that my feelings are of no concern to you." She choked out the words.

"Blast it, Adelaide. That's not what I said." But it was exactly what I'd said, wasn't it? I'd wanted to hurt her as much as she had hurt me. From the tears sliding down her face, I'd say I'd succeeded.

She sniffed. "It's what you said the day you first spied on me through my window. I should have believed you then." She tugged a black-bordered handkerchief from her pocket to wipe her tears. Her gloves tumbled to the ground, and I bent to pick them up. I held them out, and she snatched them out of my hand, pulling them on with quick, angry movements.

"Good day, Mr. Holloway." She didn't look at me as she turned and moved hurriedly down the trail. Ire filled me as I followed her back to the Library at a distance. How had our almost kiss ended with her stomping off home, still swiping at her face? Why did she never believe anything but the worst of me?

Should I try to talk to her? But what could I say? I'd already apologized, and it hadn't been enough.

Soon I stood by the iron gates and watched her disappear through the mahogany entrance doors. She slammed the door behind her, rattling the windows. Her butler poked his head out, and his confused expression turned to a frown as he spotted me.

In no mood for another dressing down, I turned towards home. I had no desire to return to my post in the woods. Our wild chase between the trees had likely scared the cat away anyways—if it had been there in the first place. But I'd need to come up with something to get ahead of the competition, because Adelaide was wrong. My feelings for her on the day I'd first climbed up to her window were miles, no worlds, apart from the way I felt about her now.

CHAPTER 15

Adelaide

Elizabeth placed the elaborate gown I would wear for the banquet on the bed and turned toward me with concern on her face. "Now don't be mad at Livvie. She didn't mean to do it. It was an accident."

Livvie could be clumsy, and although she'd broken several items in her time at the Library, she rarely handled breakables I cared about. Elizabeth's expression made me think that had changed. I furrowed my brow. "She broke something?"

"Only your confidence." Elizabeth cringed.

"Oh." I walked over to the beautiful garment laid across my bed. *Finally a gown with color!* Because of my imminent wedding, my father had declared I was to shorten the customary year of mourning him to two weeks. But tomorrow morning, Elizabeth would gather up every piece of black crape in my wardrobe and take it away never to be seen again. I ran my fingers over the bright lace and tried to remember when I'd tasked Livvie with any secret keeping.

"You had Frederick Holloway in your *bedchamber* and you didn't tell me?" Elizabeth's scandalized voice rang through the room. I turned to see her hands fisted on her hips, the proper decorum of a lady's maid entirely forgotten.

"Oh, that." My cheeks warmed.

Elizabeth's eyes raked over my face, her eyes almost bugging out of her head. "Wait, he wasn't *in* your bed was he?"

My mouth dropped open. "Of course not!"

She had the decency to look a little sheepish. "I'm sorry. His reputation isn't...stellar." She sighed. "Are you going to tell me what happened?"

I gestured to the gown. "Are you going to help me into this gown?" She rolled her eyes, and I laughed at her irreverence. Then I loosened the tasseled cord of my dressing gown, shimmied the fabric off, and tried to decide where to start. "The morning Livvie slept here, you left the window ajar..."

Elizabeth lifted the first petticoat and held it away from her body. The birdsong outside my window quieted as Elizabeth shoved the skirt over my extended arms. She tugged it in place, then pushed the second over my head.

Thick fabric shut out the room around me, and I told her everything while she arranged the yards of flowy fabric around me.

"The spell didn't keep him out?" Elizabeth's voice was muffled by the layers of lace and tulle between us. Like me, she'd heard the old Fairshaw rule her whole life.

No unwanted guest of a Fairshaw may enter, neither through door nor window.

I was the only member of the Fairshaw bloodline. I hadn't wanted to admit that I'd wanted Frederick to enter my room, but hadn't I let him hold my hand the very next day? *Before he'd kissed me.* My face heated.

"I can't fall in love." I slipped my arms into the sleeves, and let Elizabeth button up the back of the gown.

She tugged at the bodice until it was straightened to her satisfaction, then she knelt at my feet as I sat on the bed. "But you are?"

I slid my stockinged foot into the slipper. "I'm not sure. But what if I am and he doesn't find the cat? Or he does, and everything he made me feel was a lie to get to the Library?"

"I don't think there's a way to truly know his intentions, *or* who will find that cat, Adelaide." I'd been afraid of that. But what would I do if either scenario happened? How could I have let my feelings carry me away like this?

"You won't punish Livvie, then?"

It took me a second to understand what Elizabeth was asking. I stared aghast at her. "Have you ever known me to punish anyone for anything?"

She laughed. "No. And it probably makes you a terrible mistress." My father had said the same thing. He had probably been right, but I wasn't going to heed the words of a man who had left me to be sold off like fattened cattle to the highest bidder.

I stood, and as I twirled, my skirts danced around me. "This doesn't need any alterations, does it?"

Elizabeth shook her head. "It's perfect."

The dress might be perfect, but I could drum up no excitement for the event it had been tailored for. I'd wear this confection of a dress at the banquet tomorrow night. I was thankful to no longer have to wear the stiff, flat fabrics that made up my mourning clothes. But the mere thought of the desperate men searching for the Fairshaw Cat entering my home to gawk at me, made anxiety snarl and tighten around my windpipe.

I let my fingers slide over the blue silk that brought out the same shade in my eyes. I looked regal in the gilded mirror Elizabeth held. If Frederick was at the banquet, would his eyes light up at the sight of me in something other than black? Or would he ignore me like he had at the market?

And why did I care?

He'd all but told me he'd only saved me to protect his own interests. I shouldn't want to speak to him again. I pressed a hand to the treacherous organ that beat under the smooth fabric of my gown. Mr. Holloway's grin might flip my stomach, but that didn't mean I must let him get away with it.

Chapter 16

Adelaide

The large table in the Fairshaw kitchens groaned under the weight of the spread covering it. Or perhaps the groan was my own as I surveyed the mouthwatering feast. Tarts and pies of every kind. Fragrant roast meat and pickled vegetables. Fresh rolls and herbed butters.

The large ovens had been fired up since dawn, and the heat in the room was stifling. Since sunrise, I'd worked tirelessly alongside the servants, but soon dusk would fall and we'd see the fruits of our labor. I wiped sweat off my brow with a handkerchief finally not lined with black, and turned to the housemaid behind me.

"M'lady, will these suit you?" The girl, not much older than Livvie, held out a pale pink tablecloth. The damask pattern shone in the light from the lamps.

They weren't the right color for the flower arrangements. At all. "I think the pale blue ones would do better. Do you know if they can be ready by tonight?"

"I will see to it that they are, M'lady." She curtsied, and I returned to peruse the food in front of me. I'd overseen banquets at the Fairshaw Library from the time I was a child, and the many tasks involved were as natural as breathing. But this one wasn't like the others we'd hosted. This banquet was specifically for the participants in the hunt for the Fairshaw Cat. Why they'd need one was beyond me, but my father had had it written down as he lay on his deathbed, so here I was, preparing a banquet for my future husband and his competitors. A band tightened around my lungs, restricting my breathing.

"Your bath is ready, M'lady." Elizabeth peeked in through the servant's passage.

"Give me a minute, please, Elizabeth."

"Of course, M'lady."

She dipped back out, and I turned to the housekeeper. "Have I covered everything, Mrs. Tabor?"

"For the banquet, sure. But, M'lady, you look a fright. No way to meet your prospects, that's for sure. I think you should go have that bath Miss Masfield has ready for you, and we'll take care of everything else here."

I sighed. No one like our trusty old housekeeper to remind me exactly why I'd held off on getting ready. I had no interest in being paraded in front of a hall full of townsfolk desperate to get their hands on the cat, and by extension, me. "Thank you, Mrs. Tabor. I'll certainly take that into account." With one last glance at the mouth-watering feast, I pushed open the doors, and left the kitchen and its oppressive heat.

The banquet was underway. Dressed in a gown the color of a summer sky, I sat at the table and tried not to choke on my soup. The rapt attention of every man in the hall made it difficult. Anxiety clamped like a vice around my ribs, and I lowered my spoon.

I'd greeted my guests at the door as was customary. Since, I'd mingled with what had to be every man in Fairshaw. Merchants I'd spoken with at market, scholars that visited the Library daily, even men from the poorer classes I'd had no interaction with. The banquet was not a requirement for the participants in the hunt, but it was clear that most of the guests hoped hints would be dropped during the party. There were also those who hadn't thought that far, but weren't in a position to refuse a free meal. After the twentieth covert question, and a few not so covert ones, about the whereabouts of the cat, I learned to smile demurely and excuse myself from the conversation. But as I'd looked into the faces of men young and old, one had been missing. *Why wasn't he here?* I'd hoped he hadn't meant his cruel words in the woods two days ago, but maybe he had. *Maybe he truly was the scoundrel I'd named him the day we met.*

The din of silverware clinking against porcelain drew me back to the hall. I caught the eye of a leering gentleman twice my age, and averted my gaze as the soup curdled in my stomach. He was one of the ones who'd asked me outright what he needed to do to find the Cat. I'd quickly bowed out of the conversation. I didn't have any hints to drop, and if I did, I wouldn't have. *Maybe, just maybe, I could go my whole life without the cat being found. Was that too much to hope for?*

I didn't want to get married, not if it meant losing my independence. And as much as I enjoyed the careful preparation and execution of a successful party, this one in particular was stealing precious time away from my last days of freedom. If I could make it through three more courses, I was certain I'd be able to slip away unnoticed during the dessert.

"This is a wonderful celebration, Miss Fairshaw. I commend your choice of soup." A gentleman to my right leaned forward. I recognized him as one of my father's acquaintances.

"Thank you, Mr. Winterbottom, I will be sure to pass

your compliments to the cook." I sent him a stiff smile, and tried to look anywhere else when he sent me an overly friendly one in return.

Just three more courses.

You can do three more courses.

The flavor of the rhubarb tart danced on my tongue as I finally crept through the halls toward my bedchamber. If I could only make it to the vine, I would be safe. I'd received my fair share of sullen glances as it had become clear there would be no clues to help anyone find the cat tonight. But as the food and drinks had continued to appear in front of the guests, the frowns had eased.

My heavy skirts swished as I tucked them out of the way of the closing door. I didn't dare try to get out of this gown on my own, but the vine should be easy enough to slip onto without trouble, even in this monstrosity of a garment.

I strode across the dark room and opened the window, raising my skirts and pushing them out ahead of me. Good thing I didn't have company. Elizabeth would be scandalized to see me uncover myself like this. My skin didn't show, but ladies didn't flaunt their underwear, however much it covered. *Desperate ladies escaping dinner parties they didn't care to attend were the exception.*

"Miss Fairshaw, what on earth are you doing?" Frederick's voice cut through the quiet of the night, and I let out a panicked squeak.

"What in God's name are you doing here?" I barely pushed the words past the heart thrashing in my throat.

His frowning face came into view. "Aren't you supposed to be at your banquet? It's all anyone's talked about in town for days."

"I could ask the same of you!" I hissed the words as I tugged on the fabric of my skirts to pull them back into my room.

A sound from the hall made me still. If I didn't get out now, I'd never get away. Worse, what if someone came upon me like this, with my dress hanging out the window and the rest of me in a state of undress? And in the company of a man? I cursed. I had no choice but to keep going. I pushed my arm out past the mass of fabric and frills. "I need your help. My dress is stuck. Can you pull me out?"

"What? Are you out of your mind?"

"Please, Frederick." I heard him shift at the same time as the sound in the hall revealed itself as footsteps. Then his strong hand wrapped around mine, and a quick tug later, I was outside my window and pressed against

Frederick's hard side. The footsteps on the other side of my door halted just as I reached in to shut the window. "Quick, help me up so I'm out of sight!"

"I've got you." Strong hands wrapped around my waist as Frederick hefted me onto the vine out of sight from the window and scrambled after me. The muffled creak of my bedchamber door sounded on the other side of my closed window. I'd made it.

Our heavy breaths filled the air, but even if someone were to cross the room and glance out the window, they wouldn't see anything out of the ordinary. Nor would the sound of our conversation filter down. Only Elizabeth knew of my secret, and she wouldn't break my confidence.

The moon sailed out from behind a cloud, and I glanced at the man by my side, wiggling away a little as I realized how close we sat. "Thank you for your help, Mr. Holloway."

He gave a nod, and I suddenly remembered how deeply his words had cut outside the ruins in the Fairshaw woods as he'd told me I was nothing more to him than soon-to-be property. And now I was trapped in his company. I couldn't sneak back inside until the banquet was well and over, or someone might come looking for me and then drag me back there.

Frederick shifted next to me. "Are you going to tell me why you're sneaking out of your window in the middle of your own party?"

"Are you going to tell me why you didn't even attend?"

His smirk in the moonlight flipped my stomach. "Did you look for me at your banquet, Miss Fairshaw?"

I rolled my eyes. "You're sitting outside my window, it's hard to confuse a hop branch with the Fairshaw Library's banquet hall."

He tsked and tilted his nose skyward, his voice nearly unrecognizable. "I'm pleased to inform you that I indeed attended your feast, Miss Fairshaw. The soup was quite delicious, though I found myself partial to the meat pies."

His imitation could have fit any number of my guests tonight. It made me snort with laughter, despite the anger simmering in my blood. "I'm so glad to be out of there. I wish I hadn't had to spend the better part of a week preparing for it."

Frederick flicked a green leaf back and forth with his finger, then tilted his chin towards me. "What else would you do? Are wealthy heiresses busy?"

Of course he'd ask that. I curled my fists into the silky material of my evening gown, pushing down my annoyance. "There's so much I want to accomplish while I still have the chance. Once the cat is found, I'll be married and my freedom will be gone for good."

A sound of disbelief sounded beside me, and when I turned, the moonlight sharpened the emotion on his handsome face. "I'm not going to lock you up!"

"And if you don't find the key?" I raised an eyebrow, daring him to prove me wrong.

"Then you should still expect a husband, not a jailor."

I huffed. "Just like a man to assume there's a difference for a woman."

"I, for one, just helped you escape your hostess duties. Surely that puts me a step above the rest?"

My lips twitched. "Providing your intentions were good, yes. But you haven't explained why you were prowling the vines outside my window in the first place. It's not the most proper of pastimes, is it?"

"I wasn't prowling." I stared at him until his cheekbones darkened. A quick burst of victory filled my chest. *So he did have a sense of decorum after all.* He cleared his throat. "I wanted to talk to you."

"For someone who merely wants to own me, you seem to want to talk a lot."

"When did I say I wanted to own you?"

I threw my hands up. "Isn't that what this whole thing is about? Every man of marrying age trying to find a cat so they can own the Fairshaw Library, the surrounding land, and me? You've made it clear enough you desire the same."

"When?"

"After you rescued me in the woods?"

He flinched. "I should never have said that. It's not how I feel about you."

His voice was sincere, but he was just one man. There were so many others searching for the cat alongside him. Like the old gentleman seated across from me in the banquet hall, whose watery eyes had tried to catch mine all evening. I shuddered. "I just want to be allowed to say no."

Frederick stayed quiet for so long I wondered if he'd heard me at all. But maybe he didn't care. *Why would he?*

"I'm sorry." He cleared his throat. "And for what it's worth, Miss Fairshaw, when I'm your husband, that will be your right."

CHAPTER 17

Adelaide

My cheeks were on fire. I hadn't meant to be so honest. Frederick wasn't my friend, as much as he'd claimed he wanted to be. He may have saved me from discovery by whoever had entered my room, and I might enjoy his company more than I ought to. But if I'd let my eyes linger on the width of his shoulders, or held his mesmerizing gaze a little too long, that was no reason to think I could trust him.

His finger touched my chin and gently tipped my face towards his. "I'd be lying if I said I didn't want to find the cat for the riches it will bring. Seeing your sisters waste their youth and strength on constant labor will do that to a man. But I wish you had the freedom to choose your husband."

I nodded. "Thank you." Silence fell around us again,

and propped on my trusty hop vine, with the moon above and the rest of the world hidden in darkness, my shoulders sank. I closed my eyes and rested my head against a lumpy part of the vine. Exhaustion pulled at me. *I needed to get inside before I fell asleep out here.*

"I should go." My garbled words crushed the silence.

"Do you need my help to get back into your room?" Frederick's voice rumbled against my cheek.

"I think so."

"Okay. Let me know when you're ready." His warm breath caressed my temple, and the sensation felt off. Why was he… He shouldn't be this close, should he?

I opened my eyes, and my lashes brushed his chin. I gasped and pulled away, grabbing the vine behind me so I didn't jolt myself completely off the branch. "What are you doing?"

"I'm not doing anything, Miss Fairshaw. You fell asleep on me." He grinned, and the light in his eyes made mortification burn hotter in my cheeks.

I groaned. "Why didn't you wake me up?"

He shrugged. "You looked so peaceful. I figured you needed sleep."

"How long was I out?" Was it late enough servants had come to my room and discovered my bed empty? *Oh, please, don't let anyone have found me missing from my bed!*

That would be the talk of the town for sure, and I'd never hear the end of it from Mrs. Tabor.

"Long enough I'm afraid your guests have all left. If you give me your hand, I'll help you down." His warm hand clasped mine, and a moment later, without ripping the fabric of my dress, I'd stepped down from the vine to stand in front of my window. I opened it and paused. *There was no way I could enter my room the way I'd exited.*

"What is it?"

I hesitated while embarrassment burned hot on my face. There was no way to explain this delicately, was there? *Why hadn't I thought of this when I'd asked him to help me out?* "I...I don't know how to get back in."

I couldn't reenter my room with my skirts lowered, and I couldn't push them ahead of me as I had earlier. Not with Frederick out here. Unless...

I explained my predicament as delicately as I could, but his smirk only widened. *Why did I get the feeling this wasn't going to go the way I hoped?* "Are you going to turn around so I can crawl inside?"

He rested his elbow on the vine, and shook his head, that smirk still in place. "Don't be ridiculous. If I turn around and you slip, the fall will kill you."

Was he serious? "I can't very well undress while you're standing next to me!"

Mischief glinted in his eyes, and I already regretted my words. He cleared his throat. "I promise you'll hear no complaints from me, Miss Fairshaw."

I groaned and pressed cool hands to my hot cheeks. "You're *not* helping." *What was I going to do? He was clearly enjoying this.*

He pushed out a breath. "Okay, listen. I will help you back in, and I promise I'll keep my eyes glued to the back of your head. Satisfied?"

"How do I know I can trust you?"

He raised an eyebrow. "You don't. That's how trust works. Come now, Adelaide." He stepped so close the heat of his body scorched mine through our clothes. *I was never going to survive this.* I closed my eyes, fighting sudden light-headedness.

Don't slip.

Don't slip.

Don't slip.

I opened my eyes and lifted my skirts, the rustling silk loud in the quiet night.

"I'm not looking." His voice rumbled in my ear, some-how deeper than a minute ago.

I pushed the layers of blue silk and white petticoats through the window. Bracing my arms on the sides of the opening, I propped my knee on the sill. "Still not looking,

126

love." *Had his voice ever gone thick like this?* The deliciously dark timbre tugged at my core, and goosebumps spread across the back of my neck.

I pulled myself in through the window and…grunted as I pushed into the unyielding frame. "I'm stuck."

The length of Frederick's warm body pushed up against my back—strong, solid, and *utterly impossible to ignore.* I really hoped he wasn't peeking, because my face and ears were on fire. *Why had I thought this was a good idea?*

His hand pushed gently on my shoulder, guiding it through the window frame. His breath warmed my neck. "Tell me if it hurts."

I shivered. "It doesn't hurt, but I can't move at all." *Why did my voice sound so breathless all of a sudden?*

"I think you need to go in feet first. Come back out." He wrapped his hands around my waist and tugged, but nothing happened.

Anxiety spread in my chest, sudden, overwhelming. I whimpered as hysteria threatened to rise in my throat. *What if I couldn't get out at all? Would Frederick leave me to fend for myself, stuck halfway out of the window in the daylight, my clothes and head inside my room and the rest of me outside? My reputation would be ruined forever.*

Panic tightened around my chest, squeezing my lungs, and I gasped. "I can't. I need to keep going this way."

"Okay, we'll do it this way, then." *How was he this calm?* In another second, his hand pushed my other shoulder through the frame. I tipped forward and fell face first into my room with a small scream. The floor slammed into me, and I gasped from the pain. Somewhere above me, Frederick swore. Then his voice sounded closer, as if he was leaning through the window. "Adelaide! Are you okay?" *His irritating calmness was all gone, replaced by...fear?*

"Please *don't look*." I groaned another curse. My palms stung, and my cheekbone ached as tears sprung to my eyes.

"Are you okay? If you don't tell me you're okay *right now*, I swear to God, I'm going to look!"

"I'm fine! I'm fine. Please just turn around." Fabric rubbed against wood, and I hoped it meant he was turning away.

He let out a heavy sigh. "Tell me when you're upright?"

I pressed my sore palms to the floor and pushed myself to a sitting position. I twisted around to make sure my gown covered everything it should, and grabbed the windowsill to pull myself to my feet. "I'm upri—"

I came face to face with Frederick, and my mouth dropped open. "You... You filthy—"

"Shh." He pressed his finger to my lips. "I kept my word. I heard you pull to your feet."

"What if I hadn't been modest, yet?"

He cleared his throat. "I would have lied and told you I saw nothing. Now, are you okay? You—" He coughed, but he couldn't hide the laughter in his voice. "That was quite the entrance you made."

I stared at him, anger heating my blood. "You mean the one you didn't see?"

"You have nothing to worry about, Adelaide. I didn't—"

"If you say one more time that you didn't see anything that won't be your due when we're married, I swear on all that's holy I will *push you out* this window."

His eyes glittered. "I'm technically already outside, love."

"I *dare* you." *Blasted, infuriating—*

"I'd love to take you up on any dare you're ready to issue, love. But I have a cat to catch, so I will have to disappoint you this time. If you are quite recovered from your fall, I'll bid you goodnight."

I rolled my eyes. *Good riddance!* I turned away, but his hand wrapped around my wrist and tugged me back to the window.

His warm mouth brushed my cheek, so quick, I wasn't sure it had happened at all. "Goodnight, Adelaide."

Anger surged in my chest. "I can't believe you…" But when I turned to face him, he was gone. A minute later, the sound of boots hitting the ground drifted up from the dark below my window. I leaned out, but the moon had slipped behind a cloud, and I couldn't see him.

Hope warred with the burning anger. Why did he always leave me with this maelstrom of conflicting emotions? I'd known what I wanted until Frederick had shown up—with his appalling disregard for propriety and uncanny ability to make me laugh. I'd been so certain my deepest desire was to say no to my impending marriage. Why was it that this one, *infuriating*, man made me want to say yes?

CHAPTER 18

Adelaide

Eleven chimes rang through the night air, and disappointment weighed down my shoulders. He hadn't come.

All morning as I'd entertained the gentleman callers who waxed poetic about the weather, my father's passing, and a hundred other subjects I didn't care a whit about, I'd longed for the three chimes signifying visiting hours were over. Even Elizabeth's impeccable decorum had broken down as Stonier closed the door after the fifth pompous caller. And as I'd pictured Mr. Barr's horrified expression had he heard her, I'd dissolved into giggles as well.

But there was nothing to make me laugh out here. I shivered. The air was so much colder than I'd anticipated when I'd made my way out here. Even last night hadn't been this cool. *But then I'd had Frederick's warm body next to me.* My cheeks burned as I remembered falling asleep on him. I'd be better off heeding Elizabeth's advice and bringing my shawl next time.

Stiff from my hours of waiting, my limbs ached as I pushed off from the widest hop branch. I'd left a lamp burning on the table by my window, and I was thankful now for the warm light it dispersed as I looked around for a sturdy vine to grip on my way down.

"Leaving so soon, Miss Fairshaw?" My heart jolted as Frederick's voice sounded from the vine below me.

I tried to feign indifference, but failed spectacularly with my breathless reply. "Will you make it worth my time if I stay, Mr. Holloway?"

His deep chuckle caused magic to skitter across my skin like it had the night he'd held my hand. With a grunt, he hoisted himself up until he stood next to me on the vine. His dark eyes so warm on mine, and the planes of his face golden in the soft light from the window. "I'll guarantee it'll be worth your time, love." The timbre of his voice echoed deep in my bones, and a tremble moved through me. "Are you cold? How long have you been out here?"

His concerned voice tugged on my heart. For the first time, I dared believe he meant it for me. "A while. I'm not cold, just stiff." My teeth chattered, and he rolled his eyes.

He reached out his hand. "Come, you'll be warmer out of the wind. Unless, you wanted to go inside?" My eyes widened. Was he asking—"I meant alone, Adelaide."

My cheeks heated, and I grabbed his hand to distract myself from my blunder. The magic that tingled up my arm as his fingers curled around mine were certainly a distraction.

When we reached the vine branch, he nudged me over until we sat under the cover of a cluster of leafy vines. "This better?" I nodded, and tucked myself closer to the vine. "Does the Fairshaw magic not keep you warm?"

I wiggled my hand out of his and tucked it into the folds of my skirt. "No. The magic I was born with heals my wounds and staves off natural illness. But it doesn't keep me warm, and I can't heal others."

He nodded, then flicked absentmindedly at the bark between us. He looked out at the town beneath us, the lights this time of night were few and far between. "What about the Fairshaw Master?"

I hesitated, and he turned and sent me a sidelong glance that made my heart beat faster. *Why did his attention affect me like that?* "The Fairshaw Master is different. His power and wisdom is unmatched. He can use his magic to heal others, and turn it according to his wishes."

Would Frederick wield the magic better than my father had? Or would the power make him distant and pretentious, too? *Was I making a mistake in telling him this?*

"Other families have magic, too, of course, but not like ours."

Frederick leaned back against the vine. His expression was lost to the darkness around us, but his voice was soft and dreamy. "I can't wait. What does it feel like?"

I let out a deep breath. "I don't know what it feels like to be the Fairshaw Master, but the magic I have..." I slid my hand along the vine between us until I found his. My heart thundered in my chest as I slipped my fingers around his warm, calloused hand—so unlike those of the gentlemen who'd called on me earlier today. Theirs had looked as soft and white as my own, where Frederick's was tanned and strong from hours of labor out of doors. I ran the pad of my thumb over a puckered scar. His quick intake of breath made my heart jump, but it wasn't what I'd meant to show him.

"It feels like this." I brushed a finger over the inside of his wrist. He shivered under my touch, and when he spoke my name it was but a breath.

I pulled my hand back as if his skin had burned me. Above us the moon slipped out from behind a cloud. "Is...Is that what it feels like when *I* touch you?" *Where was the cocky man I'd met less than a fortnight ago? Who was this man whose eyes burned as he looked at me?*

I swallowed, and my voice trembled. "Yes." He leaned

closer, and my pulse skittered erratically. "Frederick, what are you doing?"

"I want to kiss you."

My face heated, and I couldn't look at him. "I can't."

He pulled back, nodded. "Okay."

Desperate to fill the silence between us, I blurted out the first question I could think of. "Have you come any closer to finding the cat?" His body stiffened, but he didn't answer. Disappointment tugged away the last of my embarrassment. *He wanted to kiss me, but he couldn't give me any updates on whether or not he'd seen the cat?* "Are you even looking for it?"

He huffed. "How can you ask that? I only ever come to see you when it's too late to see anything in the woods."

Hope thrilled in my heart, even as his annoyance grated. Why didn't he understand that our relationship could go nowhere unless he found it? What would I do if he didn't? I shivered, the night suddenly twice as cold against my heated skin.

Concern slipped into his voice again. "Are you cold?" I shook my head, but he wrapped his arm around my shoulder. When had I moved so close to him? "Come here, Adelaide. I won't kiss you, but I'm not going to let you freeze to death when I'm right here."

He tugged on my shoulder again, and I relented, letting

him tuck me into his side. *He was so warm, and so solid.* I sighed, and leaned into him. His chuckle rumbled through his torso. I smiled and tucked my face against the fabric of his coat. *Would I ever feel this comfortable again?*

"How do you feel now?"

He brushed a kiss against my hair, and I sighed. "Warm."

His hot breath where his lips had been a moment ago was half a laugh, but his voice was all contentment. "Good."

CHAPTER 19

Adelaide

Hard rain pelted my window like gravel tossed against a door. But despite its angry bravado, it would bring new life to the vine climbing the old brick wall. Tomorrow, fresh shoots would sprout along the hop vine, and in a few days, tiny, cone-shaped flowers would pop out next to my window.

I wrapped the shawl closer around me and turned another page in my book. I'd been born in a magical library, but the book magic that buzzed under the surface of my skin was not just for Fairshaws.

Anyone who willed it so could open their hearts to the words on the page. The magic would swirl through their bloodstream, just like it did mine—settle deeper with each word absorbed through eyes or ears, each idea tattooed onto hearts. It was one reason my father had always allowed commoners to access certain wings of the Library.

His scorn for the lower classes had never extended to their education.

I reached blindly for the once steaming cup of tea on the table beside me and pressed the cool china to my mouth.

A boom drowned out the rain and shook me out of my thoughts as a dark silhouette filled my window, and the knock sounded again.

My heart pounded as I sat up.

A knock. It had only been a knock.

I pressed a hand to my thundering heart, willing it to calm as the large fist pressed to the glass again. *I knew that hand.* My heart did a quick jig in my chest, and a smile pulled on my cheeks. Forcing the levity from my features, I dropped my book onto the floor and reached to open the latch. I pushed the window open. "Mr. Holloway."

He looked like a drowned rat, but my heart felt light and buoyant at the sight of him. I wanted to laugh, but the man outside my window wasn't laughing. Relief shone in his eyes. "You can open your window."

It was my turn to frown. "Why shouldn't I?"

The rain dripped from the top of the windowsill onto his shoulders while the veil of drops behind him faded out the rest of the world. He rubbed a hand over his face, his expression sheepish. "Martha—my sister heard rumors that the hunt was over and your wedding was imminent. I thought maybe…"

My heart jolted sharply, but I forced nonchalance into my voice. "You were worried I was about to marry some-one else?"

"Wouldn't you care if the man who found the key was someone other than me?" The intensity in his eyes made me shrink back.

I dropped my gaze from his. A drop of water trailed his scruffy jaw, and my eyes followed the movement. What *would* I have felt if he'd come upon a locked window? If maids now streamed into my room to get me ready to marry a stranger? Dread knotted my stomach. *I would have cared more than I had any right to.*

His eyes softened and the tenderness in them sliced at my raw heart. "Adelaide, let me in."

He shouldn't call me by my given name. We couldn't afford that kind of familiarity. He had no business getting to know me—I had none letting him. I raised my gaze to tell him just that, but then he opened his mouth again. "Please."

"Frederick…"

And then, *I broke the rules.* Rules written nowhere, but that were surely implied. I was all but promised to a man whose identity was unknown—there must be rules to keep my reputation, my touch, only for him. I lifted my hand to his warm skin. He pulled in a sharp breath as my fingertips trailed his wet cheek, his stubbled jaw—found the pounding pulse in his neck.

He repeated his question, and I closed my eyes. My thumb heated under the rapid breath from his mouth. "I can't." But the words were a whimper when they ought to be a wall.

"You can, love." His full lips pressed against my fingertips, and I stepped back.

And let him in.

CHAPTER 20

Frederick

My worn boots, steeped in filth from a life far less privileged than hers, were leaving puddles on the polished floors in Adelaide's room.

And she'd let me in.

I'd fought against her walls of hostility since the day we'd met. Despite the way her eyes softened when she thought I wasn't watching and her breath caught when we touched, she'd kept me at arm's length.

I forced my hands to stay at my sides. Willed the blood pounding through my veins to settle. Adelaide's face was pale and her hands clutched at her skirts. Was she as shocked as I over what she'd done?

I'd expected to find her window locked and latched—any hope for a union between Holloway and Fairshaw gone.

But she'd let me in.

I stepped forward. Her sharp intake of breath filled my

head, heated my blood, narrowed the inches between our bodies. When I'd first climbed up to this window, I'd never expected to want her like I did—much less crave her.

My fingers closed around Adelaide's cold hands. I might be the one soaked by a spring storm, but she was the one who shivered.

I hadn't found the missing piece to a puzzle that would bring me power and magic. The Fairshaw Library was as far beyond my reach as it had ever been, but the woman I'd stumbled upon was worth a thousand libraries, and I was desperate to explore her heart. *To any extent one mind could know another, two bodies be one—I wanted all of it with her.*

The storm raged on outside, violent sprays of rain came through the open window, but neither one of us moved to shut it. I searched her eyes. Did she know *she* was the reason I'd rushed to the Library the moment I heard the cat had been found? The reason relief had coursed through my body and weakened my knees as the latch slid open under her hands?

She tilted her head to mine, and I saw my reflection in the depths of her eyes. Bending forward, I touched my chilled forehead to hers.

"Frederick." She spoke my name with such longing it quickened my breath. I slipped my hands around her waist, shut out the whispers of caution in my mind, and pulled her close.

She made a noise that was half shriek, half whimper. "You're soaked!"

I grinned against her golden hair. How did it smell like sunshine when she spent so many of her days cooped up in this Library? "Only my jacket, love. With your permission, I'll take it off."

I pulled back, and my grin broadened at her wide eyes and pinking cheeks. I shrugged off my heavy coat, and she draped it, dripping, across the chair at her desk. When she turned back to me, she stilled, uncertainty written all over her face. This moment didn't follow the careful instruction left behind by her father. She wasn't supposed to let me into her room—not when anyone could claim the key, and her, on a moment's notice.

"Who did you think had the key?" She looked so small as she asked, and I cursed her father for putting her in this position. *What kind of man made his daughter wait with bated breath to discover whether her future held happiness or horror?*

"The doctor. Ralph Harrison." She nodded, face shuttered. Was she really this indifferent? This unjust fate was hers simply because she was a woman. Had she been a man, she'd have been Fairshaw Master upon her father's death and able to choose her own life's direction. Free to choose who to invite into her life—into her bed.

Black threads of helplessness snarled around my throat until I struggled to draw air. *I wanted her. But even if she chose me, it still wouldn't matter—not unless I found the cat.*

She searched my face, her breath escaping in surprise. "You didn't want him to have found it."

I dipped my head, eyes holding hers. "I didn't."

"Why?"

I closed the distance between us, brushed my fingertips along her jaw. "You have to ask?"

She drew in a quick breath, and I leaned closer. Brushed a kiss across her bottom lip. Breathed in her sweet breath.

She shivered, blue eyes wide. "Because you want me?"

Thunder rolled outside her window, rivaling the organ in my chest. "More than that. I want to *be* yours."

Chapter 21

Adelaide

He was mine. His warm breath feathered over my lips, and the tenderest of kisses touched my mouth. My insides melted as I reached for him, sliding my hands over his warm, strong shoulders.

The dripping rain was no more as he grinned against my lips. My own smile widened, and he pulled me close—a feeling of safety settling deep in my bones. *I had no memory of ever feeling so warm, so cherished.* The rumbling thunder faded around us as he dropped another kiss to the corner of my mouth, the tip of my nose, then swallowed my laugh. *How had I ever doubted that I wanted this? Doubted him?*

Cupping the back of my head, his fingers impatiently freed my curls from the hairpins holding them captive. Shimmering magic skittered over my skin, swam through my blood, sparkled wherever his mouth touched. His warm thumb stroked my cheek, my jaw, my throat. I rested my hand against his warm neck where his pulse pounded faster than mine. Another kiss, and his teeth grazed my bottom lip.

I wanted more.

More of him.

Of this.

Magic sparkled in my veins as Frederick's heart hammered against my ribs. *But wait, I shouldn't do this, should I?* Another crash of thunder sounded outside, louder this time. *I needed to end this.*

"Frederick." My gasp was barely audible, and still he stopped.

"Yes?" He pulled back, and sharp breaths filled the air as I tried to find the words. He searched my face and dropped his hands from my waist. *When had they settled there?* "Is this too much?" *And not enough.*

"I just…" *Where was the air for the words I needed to say?*

He stepped back, hands at his sides, and an uncertain look in his eyes. "I won't rush you."

I put another step between us, smoothed the skirts of my dress and ran my fingers over my hair in a half-hearted attempt to revive my ruined chignon. "Frederick, I can't… You know I can't."

A ghost of a smile on his face. "I know you won't, if that helps."

"It's not because you're not—"

"Adelaide, I *will* find that key. I'm not letting anyone come between us." The dark promise in his eyes thrilled as much as it terrified me. How far would he go to find the key? To make me his? *If he went too far, would my feelings remain the same?*

He tugged at a disheveled curl by my ear. "I'm sorry about your hair."

I rolled my eyes, still out of breath from his kisses. From mine? "Is that all you're sorry about?"

"Did you expect me to be sorry about anything else?" The grin I'd wanted to smack off his face so many times in the past was back. *The rogue that had the ladies of Fairshaw dropping like flies.* Wasn't that what Elizabeth had called him?

How many other mouths had he kissed the way he'd just kissed mine? My face heated as reality rushed in. What had I been thinking, letting him into my room? How could I have been so foolish? To let him kiss me—and worse, kiss him back! As if we already had a future together. *As if the sparkling magic whenever we touched was anything to build a life on.*

The growing puddle on the floor drew my attention, but I didn't move to close the window. "What if another man finds the key first?"

"Then I'll take care of it." A harsh edge slipped into his

voice, and I shivered. His hand slid warm against my cheek. "I'll find the key, Adelaide, you can trust me. I'll be your husband."

I leaned my face into his hand, relishing the strength I felt there. But what if that strength led him to do the unthinkable? "I'm more worried about what you will do to find the key."

"Anything." His hand dropped from my cheek, and his eyes hardened—all the warmth gone from his voice, his smile, the air. "I'll do anything."

Gone was the man who'd touched my skin with reverence, who'd gazed into my eyes as if I held the key to his world. In his place was the one whose reputation had kept me awake at night before I knew him. *Or did I know him now? Did I really know how far he'd go in order to secure his future? Our future?*

Mr. Holloway's coat rustled as he shouldered it on. His boots tramped across the floor, and my window slid shut behind him, muffling the sounds of the storm.

What had I done? I closed my eyes, my mind an echo of the words we'd spoken minutes ago.

"Because you want me?"

"More than that. I want to be yours."

Frederick Holloway might be mine soon, but would that be enough?

CHAPTER 22

Adelaide

The words on the page refused to connect with my heart. Every bite of sliced honey cake tasted like sand, and when I sipped the freshly brewed cup of Earl Grey, I missed its soothing flavor. Closing my book, I rose, and slid it onto the shelf by my desk.

I tried not to think about the men of Fairshaw—the ones searching day and night for the cat that would decide my fate. But it was impossible to escape the rumors that swirled in the air everywhere I went. My trip to the market with Elizabeth should have served as a distraction, but as we'd passed washer ladies gathered over barrels of laundry, talking in low voices, and pointing to me, I'd lost my taste for that outing. In the kitchen, the wedding feast was all but prepared—everything set to be ready on a moment's notice. But when I ventured there, scullery maids' and housemaids' animated voices died down as soon as they noticed me.

I scanned the shelf for another volume to escape into, but I could think of nothing that would keep my attention. Again, I caught myself listening for Frederick's movements on the vine outside my window. I couldn't forget the distraught way he'd looked me over when I'd let him into my room three days ago, nor could I explain away the tenderness in his voice then. *Unless his hunt for the cat was driven by something deeper than a hunger for power?*

His quest *had* begun with a desire for wealth, I was sure of that. But was that still all he sought? His kisses had left no doubt that he wanted me, but would he still if the Fairshaw Library became his? The knowledge of the Fairshaw Library was of no use to me here. Only one person held the answers to the questions tumbling through my mind. *I needed to see Frederick, and I needed to see him alone.*

My heart pounded in my chest as I pinned my hat to the top of my chignon, found my reticule, and pulled on my gloves. Could I somehow circumvent both Elizabeth and Mrs. Tabor?

Less than a half hour later, I made my way down Pendle

Street—I didn't know where else to look for him. I rapped my gloved hand on the worn door, and a moment later it slid open. "Miss Fairshaw, is everything all right?"

My heart sank in my chest. "May I come inside, Miss Holloway?"

Frederick's sister stepped aside, and I entered the apartment that now seemed even smaller than at my first visit. She shut the door, and I turned to her. There was nothing proper about my request, but I had bypassed propriety already—first by leaving my home unaccompanied and then by visiting Pendle Street. "I need to speak to your brother, please."

Her dark eyes searched my face. Then understanding lit her features, and a soft smile bloomed on her lips. "So Liv was right, you do care for him."

I closed my eyes, pushing out a breath that left me feeling hollow. "I..."

"He's not here, Miss Fairshaw. He'll be at the docks for another hour at least. May I give him a message?" Her voice held apology, and as I opened my eyes I saw compassion on her face. Her chapped, reddened hands flattened the mended waist of the dress she wore, and I remembered her suitor from my last visit. *Did this woman know the misery of a thwarted love story?*

I could wait, but how long until he came home? And

the longer I waited, the harder my absence would be to explain to the housekeeper, who'd certainly be notified if I stayed until dark. *Why must my life be under such strict control? And how much worse would it get when I married?* Pain squeezed my heart as I swallowed. "No. I can't leave a message."

"I suppose this visit explains my brother's fervor in hunting the Fairshaw Cat." There was sadness in Miss Holloway's smile.

I longed to know that I mattered enough to Frederick that he'd look for the cat for me. Yet, as I studied my surroundings, the world he came from, how could I blame him for wanting the riches promised to the man who found it? I wanted to keep the desperation out of my voice, but it was impossible. "Do you not think he will find it?"

Again, Miss Holloway's eyes lingered on my face as if she could read my secrets. *Could she?* She sighed, a sound much too deep for a woman just a few years older than me. *How much of her youth had this life already stolen?* "If he feels for you as you do for him, I hope he does."

"Thank you, Miss Holloway." I stepped across the dirt floor towards the door, and turned to her again. "May I ask for your confidence in this matter?"

She dipped her head. "Of course, Miss Fairshaw. Does that include my brother?" I hesitated, but what good would it do if Frederick knew I'd sought him out here? I nodded and reached for the door, but before I could touch the knob, it sprang open.

"Adelaide?" Frederick stood in the doorway, surprise written on a face gray with filth. His skin was streaked with sweat and grime, and his shirt seemed more dust than fabric. I'd seen him dressed in his poor man's clothes up close only once before—every time he'd visited me, he'd been dressed like the gentleman I knew he wasn't.

A clatter sounded outside the door, followed by a sharp voice. Miss Holloway leapt forward, urgency in her voice. "Shut the door, Frederick." She squeezed herself in the gap between her brother and the door, and pushed him inside.

False cheerfulness filled her next words. "Mrs. Jones! Do you have any idea what I just heard? Molly Thompson is finally—"

She slammed the door behind her, and I was alone with Frederick.

CHAPTER 23

Frederick

I reached out for the length of cloth nailed to the wall above by the window, and pulled it down to cover the glass. Martha kept the panes clean enough you could see clear in from the outside, and I didn't need prying eyes for this. *Whatever this was.*

I stared at the highborn gentlewoman standing in my apartment. Her dress, trimmed with lace and ruffles, had not a single mended patch. Her gloves looked like they'd never been worn until this moment. What I assumed was to pass for a hat wouldn't survive a damp afternoon—of which this English coastal town offered plenty. "What are you doing here?"

"I needed to talk to you." Her voice held an edge of desperation, and still I stood rooted to the ground. I'd never expected her to show up here, and my mind struggled to join the two—the squalor of our apartment on Pendle Street and Miss Adelaide Fairshaw. The woman I'd spoken to on the vine in the dark had seemed softer some-how, more my equal. But surrounded by these bare walls and swept dirt floor, just her attire screamed the differ-ences in our stations.

Dropping her gaze, I stepped over to the pail on the stand in the corner. I splashed chilled wash water onto my face and scrubbed the filth off my hands. I grabbed the towel, and turned around with the stained rag still pressed to my face. My brows drew down. "What would be so ur-gent you needed to seek me out here?"

She wrung her gloved hands, eyes imploring me, but for what? "I need to know why you're searching for the cat. I can't stand being cooped up at the Library and not even knowing what I'm hoping for—"

"You." I cut off her rambling words. "I'm searching for the cat for *you*."

She stilled. "What? But you live *here*, and if you find the cat, the wealth of the Library will…" Her words trailed off and she watched me wide-eyed as I closed the distance be-tween us, the sound of my boots loud in the near-empty apartment.

"I know where I live, and it has nothing to do with how I feel about you." My clean palms framed her face, her trembling skin like silk under my callouses. Up close she smelled like lavender and starched lace, and I smelled like hours of toil and the stench of the docks. At the last moment I remembered the filth still on my forearms and dropped my hands. "I shouldn't touch you like this."

She huffed. "Are you worried you'll stain me?" She ripped her gloves off and tossed them to the floor as if their fate didn't concern her in the slightest. Then her warm hands were on my face, sliding over my wet jaw, along my neck where grit and sweat still mixed together.

My hands itched to wrap around her, and I closed my eyes. "Adelaide. I didn't come to the Library because I'm looking for that cat every free moment of my days. It's why I'm here now. There's still a few hours of daylight left, and I didn't want to miss any more time away from the hunt."

Not looking at her wasn't helping at all, and the gentle caress of her fingers on my neck was driving me crazy. She swallowed. "I was afraid you only wanted to win the prize for the wealth it would bring you, and seeing this place, I can't—"

I cupped her clean face in my hands, and kissed her. She tasted like hope and fancy tea, and things fairer than wealth and wisdom. Her fingers slipped up the base of my skull and into my hair. My arm wrapped around her waist, and I pulled her up against me. She gasped, and I grinned as I kissed her nose, her cheeks, her mouth. Kissed her as if she was air, and I was a man drowning. Because it was the truth. Our heaving breaths filled the room and—

Something slammed against the other side of the wall, and I jumped back from Adelaide.

"Sleeping babies, Holloway. Keep it down! That's the third time this week." The shrill voice was accompanied by a pitiful wail from the poor child she'd woken up.

I cursed. Privacy and Pendle Street didn't go together, how could I have forgotten? My gaze lingered on the woman in front of me, her pink cheeks and sparkling blue eyes, so full of life and fire. *That was why.*

"Who is that?" Adelaide's hand covered her mouth. My eyes lingered on the dark smudges that marred her porcelain-like wrists. *Had I done that?* Of course I had. She'd shown up here cleaner than I'd been in my life.

"Our neighbor." I pushed a hand through my hair. How long had Mrs. Jones listened in? Had I used Adelaide's name again? Would she put two and two together and realize who had been in my apartment alone with me? And what did she mean by the third time?

"I don't know what she's talking about. I haven't been with…no one else has been here with me since we met."

Adelaide bent to the floor and grabbed her gloves, avoiding my gaze. Her skirts rustled as they brushed the hard stamped dirt, highlighting our differences in station once again. "Does your neighbor…um, ever partake in gossip?"

I groaned. "The better question would be when she isn't."

A knock sounded at the door. Panic widened Adelaide's eyes as her head whipped up. She cast frantic glances around the room as if searching for a spot to hide. "Who is it?"

I pinned her with an incredulous stare. "How would I know?"

Regardless of who was on the other side of that door, I needed to think fast. But what options did I really have? If I hid Adelaide in Martha's bedroom it would look even more incriminating if she was found, but there was no-where else. The back door was out of the question. Any-one could lean over a fence or peek through a window and spot her. She would stand out like a sore thumb in her finery, not to mention that she was the most talked about lady in all of Fairshaw.

I grabbed her hand, pulled her over to the bedroom door, and pushed her gently inside. "Wait here."

She nodded, but looked so terrified I couldn't help but lean forward to press a kiss to her lips. "I'll get rid of who-ever it is, and I'll be back soon."

I closed the door as quietly as I could, stomped across the room, and pulled open the front door. "Frederick, I couldn't keep Mrs. Jones occupied anymore, and..." Martha entered the room and closed the door behind her. "Where's Miss Fairshaw?"

I tilted my head towards the bedroom door, and Martha's eyes widened. "Frederick James—"

I cut her off. "She's *hiding*, Martha. Why does everyone keep thinking the worst of me?"

Her eyes narrowed, and her finger poked into my chest. "Your reputation is one you've earned yourself, Frederick Holloway. Don't blame me for knowing it."

I sighed. "Right. Carry on, then."

The bedroom door creaked open behind us, and Adelaide stepped out, gloves back in place. "Frederick... Mr. Holloway. Don't let me keep you any longer."

Martha's eyes lingered on the smudged waist of Adelaide's once spotless dress. "Miss Fairshaw, your dress must have stained. Let me help you with that." She grabbed a clean towel, dipped it into the bucket of drinking water, and erased the grime from where my filthy clothes had pressed against the front of Adelaide's.

"Thank you, Martha." I pushed out a breath. "I need to get going. The cat won't catch itself." *How long since I'd arrived home? Minutes? An hour? How much more left of the daylight?* I dipped my head to Adelaide. "Miss Fairshaw, thank you for…bringing me your concerns. I'll see you soon."

I left through the back door. No reason to incite more wagging of tongues than necessary. Vaulting myself over the fence, I made my way towards the Fairshaw woods. I needed to find the cat, and I was running out of time.

CHAPTER 24

Adelaide

My visit to Pendle Street had given me as stern a talking to by the housekeeper as could have been expected. According to her, there was little more damning than making an unchaperoned visit so close to my wedding, not to mention such a visit in the poorer part of town.

"Pendle Street, Miss Fairshaw. You were spotted on Pendle Street of all places. What would you poor departed father think if he'd known a scullery maid carried news of his daughter making unchaperoned visits on Pendle Street!"

I groaned as her words echoed in my head. I'd almost grown used to the Fairshaw Cat's looming shadow over my life. But in the two days that had passed since my outing, just knowing that my last minutes of freedom were ticking away had become unbearable.

Unable to stand the walls of my room closing in on me any longer, I shut the bedchamber door behind me and strode down the halls. I ran shaking fingers over the textured frames of elaborate paintings, rubbed them across prickly, woven tapestries, and let them slide over smooth marble sculptures. I'd called this Library home my whole life, and soon it would house my husband, too—whoever he was.

I shuddered as I remembered Elizabeth's speech from yesterday. *"Word on the street is that more men are throwing themselves into the chase daily."* But why had they taken interest so late in the game? And why did every mention of it make my heart ache? Every time rumors circled that someone had found the cat, my knees wobbled like jellied broth and I found no rest until I got to my window to try the latch.

> *"Door and windows lock,*
> *until the Master of Fairshaw enters.*
> *Unimaginable riches, unparalleled power,*
> *The Fairshaw bride and Fairshaw lands,*
> *Be his alone."*

I'd heard the prophecy often enough as a child, but I'd never thought much about what it would mean for me. But with the minister as our houseguest and my wedding feast all but assembled in the kitchens, these words would soon be my life.

I halted in front of my portrait. In it I was three years old with golden hoops framing my face—light and life sparkling in my eyes. What would this child of yesteryear have thought about this misery of a cat hunt? Would she still have dared hope for the kind of romance found in the fairytales her nurse read her before bed?

I remembered Frederick's cocky speeches of riches and conquest when I'd first met him. They hadn't matched the tender way he'd kissed me in his apartment on Pendle Street. Nor had they fit the stark emotion I'd seen in his eyes as he pulled away. I touched my fingertips to my mouth and closed my eyes. *I still felt the imprint of him on my lips. Would I ever not feel it?*

Unchecked passion might not have much to do with love, but the way he'd looked at me as he'd leaned forward to kiss me? As if his eyes could touch depths within mine, and he could reach for my very soul with his? *That* was more than lust, and it made me think he'd been honest when he said he was looking for the cat for me. *And…that I wasn't alone in my heartache.*

Leaving my portrait behind, I entered the west wing of the Library. Sunlight streamed in through the high windows, and dust danced in the shafts of lights. The magic milling in the air instantly soothed me, and my shoulders lowered at the sight of shelved books from floor to ceiling. *Were they all waiting eagerly for me to pick one?* Oriental rugs swallowed the sound of my steps as I walked to the nearest shelf and pressed my cheek to the worn spines. The magic might be in the words and not the binding, but the soft leather comforted all the same. I pressed my eyes closed and let the smell of old books and ancient pine shelving soothe my frayed nerves.

I didn't know what chance Frederick had to be the winner in this chase. I did know that the moment the windows and doors shut, my mind would spring to him and only him. I'd wait breathlessly until I knew whether or not he was the new Fairshaw Master. Even as the *not* of that scenario made my heart bleed. Made me—Edward Fairshaw's daughter—jealous of Livvie, the orphan from Pendle Street.

For all the safety I'd known as a child, my meals prepared, my bed always clean and made—the thought of being forced to marry someone other than Frederick made me wish I'd been the one brought up on the docks. When Livvie one day met a man she cared for, she'd be free to be with him. He'd need only prove his love and faithfulness, and not the arbitrary skill of sniffing out magical pets.

I pressed closer to the shelf and listened for the thrumming song that only those who read could hear—like a great uprising of voices and thoughts cemented in ink. The same lulling melody that had rocked me to sleep every night since the one when I'd breathed my first breath and my mother her last. I pulled on a beloved volume until the shelf let it go, searching the words of each page as if they might hold the answer to my predicament right there in black ink on yellowed paper.

Instead I heard Frederick's question again. *"Wouldn't you care if the man who found the key was someone other than me?"*

If he only knew the agony it was to pretend daily tasks had any sort of meaning while I waited to see who would own my fate, he wouldn't have had to ask. I replaced my book on the shelf and straightened to search for another.

A wave of pain crashed into me, and I staggered. Clutching the shelf beside me, I looked down to search for the rip in my dress, my chest, the life blood surely pouring forth—but found none. Then nausea rose so suddenly, so violently, in my throat that I clapped my free hand to my mouth.

I leaned against the bookshelf behind me and gasped for air—but before I could call for help, the sensation disappeared. Only the crushing weakness in my bones stayed as I straightened. *How could I be sick? The Fairshaw magic in my veins had kept me healthy all my life. Had these last days of little sleep and no appetite finally gotten to me?* I moved along the halls of the Library, where magic should have restored me, but I couldn't shake the weakness weighing down my limbs.

I forced my feet to lift for each stair step until I reached the floor where my bedchamber was. Finally in my room, I sank against the closed door.

I needed to call for Elizabeth. She'd bring me hot tea and toast. Maybe after the food, I could nap. *Oh, how Frederick would tease me if he found me in bed during the afternoon again.*

A rap sounded at the window. As if thinking of him had made him appear, Frederick knocked again. From my spot on the floor I took in his lowered brows and the tight line of his mouth—his worry palpable. "Adelaide." His shout muffled through thick glass. My limbs trembled as I got to my feet and crossed to the window. "Adelaide, are you sick? Why were you slumped on the floor like that?"

"I'm well, Frederick." I meant it—the nausea had faded at the sight of him.

"You don't look well. Let me in." I put my hand on the latch and pushed it aside.

It didn't move.

The metal simmered with magic, and sparks shocked my fingers. I yelped and pulled my hand away from the burning pain.

"What's wrong?" Frederick's voice came as if from miles away through the glass.

Terror crushed my lungs, and my mind spun—so fast.

The window was locked, but not by me.

By magic.

Which meant only one thing.

I lifted my gaze to the man I loved desperately, hoping against hope that his answer could remove the horrible ache spreading in my chest. "Frederick? Did you come here because you found the cat?"

But even as I voiced the question, I knew the answer. If he had come here as the Library Master, the latch would have opened for him.

And it hadn't.

CHAPTER 25

Adelaide

The stricken look on Frederick's face sent a terrible ache through my chest. "It's locked." My words were a whisper, but he didn't need to hear them.

His eyes. Oh, his eyes slayed me. The pain I read there as my words came through the glass felt like a fatal wound must—crushing, splintering, pain. "Adelaide, I—"

"It doesn't matter." I strove to keep my voice steady, fought the stars at the edges of my vision, mentally scrambled away from the panic rising. "I have to marry the man who found the key. It doesn't matter who he is." *It didn't matter. Not at all.* The only thing that mattered was that it wouldn't be Frederick.

It wouldn't be him.

I'd wanted… I'd hoped.

Visions I'd never allowed myself to have sprouted before my mind's eye.

Frederick's arms around me as he tucked me close to his

chest, the great train of my wedding gown trailing behind us. Our laughter echoing off the walls in the Library hallways as we walked away from our ceremony.

Tow-headed children running through the sun-filled Library gardens, their calls of "Papa" muffled by Frederick's laughter as he scooped them up, peppering kisses over their golden curls and laughing faces.

The vision faded, leaving behind an ache I didn't think I'd survive. We'd lost. Defeat pounded through my veins as my soul shriveled into something hard and black.

"Don't... Don't do anything." Frederick's voice was pleading. "I will fix this. I'll be back." I nodded weakly, staring at the spot where he'd been before he dropped from view. *He couldn't fix this.*

Waves of grief struck my body, battered it until I could no longer feel them, or it. Numbly, I watched as my door flew open and Elizabeth stormed in. Followed by the dressmaker, by Livvie, and a slew of servants I could no longer place.

My room filled with a flurry of activity. Shining eyes, wide smiles, and excited chatter. Someone took my hand, and I was pulled, gently, but firmly through the halls to the room where a maid lifted my wedding gown down from the wall. Livvie's small hands ran over the train, and her eyes shone with happiness. *She had no idea this would kill her brother.* I closed my eyes as another sharp pain tore through my chest.

Buckets of steaming water poured into the tub. Hands undid ribbons and laces until I stood in front of my bath naked as the day I was born, my privacy completely forgotten. But did it matter? These women loved me, had seen to my baths since I was a curly-headed babe. And soon I'd be as vulnerable in front of a stranger—my boundaries, too, a thing of the past.

I climbed into the tub. "Shut your eyes before I pour!" I closed my eyes only a moment before water plastered my hair to my head.

"No, not like that! Have her lean her head back first. Her hair will be nothing but tangles."

I tilted my face to the ceiling as hands pushed my soggy hair off my face. More hot water. Elizabeth picked up my hand, scrubbing my nails with a brush. Was dirt from the hop vine stuck under them? *Oh, what I'd give to be on that vine with Frederick. What I'd give to be anywhere with him, and not here, being made ready to marry another.*

"Okay, come on out of there." Hands that weren't mine rubbed water off my body until my skin burned. Silky garments were tugged over my head, ribbons threaded. The heavy gown slipped down my body. I glanced at the gems covering the bodice, the sparkly lace of my sleeves, and felt nothing. No joy for the beautiful gown wrapping around me. No sadness from losing Frederick.

My wet hair was dried and curled into long ringlets. Someone pushed a wreath of flowers over my head. I let them do what they wanted. It didn't matter anymore. Nothing mattered.

I was a prize for my father's successor, and I'd been a fool to let my heart warm to another. Frederick might have convinced himself he'd be the winner in this competition—but *I* should have known better than to believe in luck. Or was it destiny? Whatever he believed in, it had failed us, and we'd both pay for my foolishness.

"You're crying." Elizabeth wiped a tear from my cheek. "That's no look for a bride?" *But I wasn't a bride—I was a pawn in a game. A thing to be won and used.* Brides were loved, honored, cherished. I would be none of those things.

"Your cheeks are like a waterfall! You need to stop or your eyes will swell!" A housemaid much younger than me pressed cool cloths to the tops of my cheeks.

"Adelaide, you don't know who it is, do you?" Elizabeth again. I shook my head. She frowned, and then her eyes softened with understanding. "You wanted it to be Frederick." If she could make out the answer in my sob, it was only because she already knew my heart. She

171

wrapped her arms around me, and I let my forehead drop to her shoulder. "You can't know it isn't him, can you?"

"He was there." I wheezed. "When the window locked." I looked up at her, and the pity on her face wrenched away the last of my self-control.

She tucked me into her chest as heaving sobs wracked my body. Her hands rubbed hard circles on my back, as if she could rub the ache away. When nothing could, and nothing ever would. "I'm so sorry, love."

CHAPTER 26

Frederick

I scrambled down the vine, jumped too soon, and slammed my knees against the ground below. The sharp pain in my bones had nothing on the one in my chest. I wanted Adelaide Fairshaw to be mine, library or no library. *Why did she have to be a blasted Fairshaw!* If she'd had any other name, I could have courted and married her today.

If she'd had any other name, you wouldn't have known her.

I pushed that truth to the back of my mind, rose from the ground, and ran. I didn't have a plan. My thoughts were muddled, except for one. *I needed to find the cat, or whoever had found it.* What I'd do when I found it wasn't important. I'd figure that out then. I couldn't stand idly by while the woman I loved—yes, loved—was married off to a stranger. Not when I was certain she returned my feelings. If her visit the other day hadn't made it clear, her stricken eyes as she found her window locked, had.

I trawled the city forward, backwards, across. Questioned preoccupied strangers and eager-to-please schoolboys. Followed long forgotten trails in the woods. Until I stood in a forest grove gazing at a small, furry body.

I was certain the animal in front of me wasn't alive, but why had the man who had found the Fairshaw Cat, killed it?

Closing the distance between me and the lump of matted fur, I dropped to my haunches. I inspected the feline's ravaged throat, and the glimpse of silver above the deadly wound was like a punch to my gut.

Surely it couldn't be... But as I stretched out my fingers to touch the bloodstained leather collar, magic pulsed through the air. My fingertip touched the shimmering key, and a moment later, the cool metal pressed into my palm.

I stared at the object in my tingling hand, unable to comprehend this new reality. If a man had hurt the cat, he would have been a fool to leave the key behind. I didn't think a magical creature like the Fairshaw Cat could be killed by wild animals, but what other explanation was there?

Leaving the beautiful cat behind in a ditch like this warred with a sense of justice I hadn't known I had. Unease skittered across my skin, leaving goosebumps in its wake, and I longed for the Fairshaw Master's healing pow-ers. *But even then I wouldn't have been able to raise it from the dead.*

I turned away, clutching the small silver object in my hand. I had no time to lose—the heartbreak in Adelaide's eyes beckoned from across town. She must be out of her mind with worry, and I desperately wanted, *no needed*, to soothe her fears. That day we'd met, she'd balked at the thought of marrying me—but today, I didn't think she would.

CHAPTER 27

Frederick

I'd won. My prize stood before me, draped in lace that sparkled like sun over frosted cobblestones. Adelaide Fairshaw was magnificent—far more beautiful now than on the day we'd met. One look at her, and I didn't care about the powerful magic I'd begun this journey to own.

Didn't care that the knowledge and wealth surrounding me, the vivid tapestries, or ornate carvings of wood and marble were mine.

It didn't matter that I was the master of this place which the word grandeur didn't quite do justice.

My boots had trod a dirt floor on my best day, my bare feet hit cobblestone on my worst. Enough had seldom been my lot, but neither the wealth nor magic I now possessed gave me the thrill that her rapt eyes on mine could.

Pale lashes rested against high cheekbones. Any moment now, she'd lift her blue eyes to mine and know that *she* was the real prize—that the riches of the Library didn't hold a candle to *her*.

But she didn't meet my eyes. Not burning with anger, not darkened with desire, not sparkling with mirth.

I frowned. *Was she afraid of me?* She had to know I'd do nothing to hurt her. I held out my hand, and for a moment she hesitated. Her hand was as soft and warm as I remembered, but the way it rested limply in mine was new. "Adelaide? What is wrong?"

Her eyes met mine then, and the grief in the blue depths was a kick to my gut. *Did she not want to marry me after all?* Her gaze returned to the floor, and doubt swirled like a storm in my belly. Something was very wrong, but there was no time to explore it. She was dressed for our wedding, and every servant in her, our, employ lined the walls of the small chapel in the Library's west wing where we stood.

The minister stepped forward. "You are ready, Master Fairshaw?"

I needed to talk to my bride. I needed to find the Adelaide that had melted into my arms just days ago. What had happened to turn the horror-stricken woman I'd left inside her locked bedroom into the stony one at my side? *No, I wasn't ready.* "Yes, sir."

I clasped Adelaide's lifeless hand in mine and walked

her to the front of the chapel. It wasn't the way I'd imagined our wedding. Adelaide might be here in the flesh, more gorgeous than in my dreams, but there was no laughter in her eyes, no quick smiles or longing glances sent my way. *Had her visit to Pendle Street alienated her?* No, that couldn't be it. She'd referred to me as dock trash too often in our early acquaintance to not know the life I'd led.

My thoughts continued to churn throughout the ceremony. The minister needed to ask me twice if I'd lay down my life for Adelaide's. I cleared my throat and repeated the vow. "...and also lay down my life for her."

"Will you stay with her all your days, cherishing her..." His monotone voice droned on, but I couldn't pay attention. Had everyone in attendance imagined the wedding of the Fairshaw Master to his bride to be a miserable, absentminded affair? They must have. It wasn't supposed to be a pairing of love, after all. Was my dark mood and Adelaide's downcast eyes exactly what they'd expected?

They might have, but I hadn't. I'd wanted to marry the Adelaide who'd melted under my touch. Who'd asked questions no one else had, whose desire to know my every thought was the aphrodisiac I'd never known I needed. But that woman was missing.

As we faced each other, our gazes should have locked. But my bride stared straight ahead in quiet resignation to marry whomever had proved worthy to be the Fairshaw Master. At the prodding of the man forging our lives together, I pressed a kiss to the unmoving lips of a woman I knew was alive but who didn't respond.

The Adelaide Fairshaw I had met that first day would have drawn blood from my lip before she'd conceded to marry a man she despised. She'd have shot daggers at me with eyes that sparked with the fire of injustice, not let me hoist her limp body into my arms.

I carried her close to my chest as servants' cheers rose behind us. The intoxicating scent of her hair wrapped around my senses, but it couldn't shake my worry. I'd seen the terror in her eyes when she'd realized she'd be forced to marry another. How was she now my wife and her strongest emotion resignation?

I lowered my bride to the floor inside the doors of the Library Master's bedchamber—our bedchamber. The moment that had haunted my dreams should have had nothing on reality.

But did.

In place of the passion I'd imagined, I stood in front of a shell of the woman I loved. "Adelaide, talk to me. Why won't you look at me?" Her beautiful eyes finally met mine, and welled with tears. The sight gutted me. "Don't you want me as your husband?"

"I did."

The past tense in her words tore at me. What had happened in the scant hour I'd been away? "But you don't now?"

She closed her eyes, and her lashes pushed the first tear down her cheek. I folded her into my arms, and she rested her cheek against my chest. I pressed a kiss to her hair.

I needed to get to the bottom of her unease, not let her deep exhale as she pressed closer sway me to tighten my arms around her. Moisture seeped through my shirt, reminding me this was an embrace of comfort, not passion.

I bent to kiss the tears from her cheeks, but when she offered her mouth, I didn't hesitate—couldn't hesitate.

Hot embers glowed to life at her kiss, and relief flooded my body. She might have changed her mind about marrying me, but she wanted me still.

The hands that had barely held on to mine during our ceremony now pushed through my hair, tugging at the strands, and making me groan. Fire roared at the flick of her tongue against mine, burning hotter with her gasp as I lifted her off the ground.

Her smooth skin under all that lace far surpassed the dream. She sighed into me, her sweet breath and soft hands everything I'd waited for. And as her body pressed into mine, and for the first time since I'd found the ravaged Fairshaw Cat on the side of the road, the weight of unease lifted.

I felt at peace.

Chapter 28

Adelaide

Sleep held me tight in its embrace as I fought to claim wakefulness. *When had I dozed off?* I tried to remember the hazy moments before unsettling dreams had claimed me.

I opened my eyes only to find I was immobilized by a muscled forearm, not sleep. Remembering why I'd slept in his arms made my cheeks heat. Just for a moment I let myself relish the warmth of his chest snug against my back. *I never wanted to move.* Then nausea rose up, sudden and strong.

"Frederick?" His answer rumbled against my back. I gasped, pulling frantically at his arm. "I'm not feeling well." I crawled out of his embrace and made it to the edge of the bed at the last minute.

When the horrible retching stopped, I sank back against Frederick. He let go of my hair, then reached behind him and handed me his shirt. I took it, then hesitated. *Why was I holding his shirt?*

"Wipe your mouth." His voice was gentle.

"But, your shirt—" He took the shirt from my hands, dabbed it at my chin and the corners of my mouth. I winced at the orange stains on the crisp fabric, then shivered as cold sweat slicked my body. Frederick tugged on the sheets until he could wrap one around me, then tucked me against his warm chest, covering both of us with the blankets. "Should I call for the doctor as well as a scullery maid?"

Weak by the tremors, I didn't want to speak, but the thought of shaking my head had my stomach roiling again. "No. Please don't."

Frederick kissed the top of my head and spoke into my hair. "Were you...nervous?"

I frowned. "Why would I—" Embarrassing clarity struck, and I couldn't speak past the mortification.

"I thought maybe... You didn't even want to talk to me after the wedding, and this morning you threw up, so—"

"No!" My cheeks burned, and I wanted to melt into the blankets and disappear. *Thank God, he couldn't see my face!* "No, I wasn't nervous."

"Then what? You told me Fairshaws can't catch common illnesses, so that can't be it."

There was no holding off on this discussion. I couldn't

hide my decision, not when I needed to distance myself from him. Letting him comfort me last night had been a mistake. I couldn't allow myself to love a murderer—not when the Fairshaw magic might act on my feelings. "What did you have to do to get the key?"

He stiffened behind me. "What?"

"What did you do to the person who had the key first?"

The breath he let out behind me cooled my damp neck. "Nothing, I—"

"Don't lie to me." I sat up and turned to face him. "I was there when the doors closed, which means that someone had the key, and it wasn't you. I saw your eyes as you left…" I shuddered. "You said yourself you'd do anything to get the key, and then you returned an hour later, key in hand. What am I supposed to think?" I threw my hands up, moving fully out of his embrace. "*No one* would give up the key while alive!"

"You're right about that." He mumbled the words under his breath, but their implication was deafening.

My heart dropped so low I could no longer feel it. I watched the shadows creep over his face as waves of disgust and helplessness crashed through my body. *He'd killed someone.* My new husband had killed for the Fairshaw Library, for me. *I couldn't live with a murderer.* Couldn't love one.

You already love him.

I pressed my hands against my face as if my shaking fingers could press the love away. *Oh, if only!*

"Adelaide." He groaned my name and reached for me, but I moved away. "You won't let me hold you?"

I shook my head and looked into the angry face of the man I shouldn't love. What terror would I bring down over the town of Fairshaw if I let my feelings remain as they were? I swallowed the tears tingling against the back of my eyes. I was going to retch again.

I longed for his strong, perfect, work-worn hands to touch me, hold my hair back, tuck me into his warm embrace. But in my imagination they dripped with innocent blood. My voice shook. "I don't want your hands on me."

My eyes moved to his face, and I wanted to curl up into a ball at the hurt I saw there. This was worse than the Frederick Holloway I'd met that first day, who'd all but leered at the thought of owning me. His hard eyes speared me, his mouth set in a snarl. "That's how it's going to be? You won't let me tell you the truth?"

"You're trying to lie to me! There's no way anyone would have found the key and given it to you, and you were with me when the window shut!"

Jaw clenched, he rose from the bed, tugged on his trousers, and let the door slam behind him. In his wake, the crystal vase on the table rattled, fell to the floor, and shattered. *It had nothing on my heart.*

I lost another battle with nausea. But this time when the spasms ceased,

I was alone.

CHAPTER 29

Frederick

I was the Fairshaw Master, and the prize I'd worked so tirelessly to achieve was mine. There may have been other things I'd come to desire that I didn't have, but at least I had this. *Finally, my sisters would no longer have to work their fingers to the bone.*

I'd left the bride who wouldn't as much as look at me and gone straight to the housekeeper to arrange for Martha's new rooms. My sister had refused the accommodations, but not the purse of coins I'd handed her next. I'd let Liv move in in her stead and told her to stay away from her duties. She could sleep past sunrise now.

Having to be consulted about staff I struggled to tell apart was still a challenge. It didn't help that I didn't understand half of what I was responsible for. The magic I was supposed to have also seemed to be missing. It buzzed in the air around me and under my hand whenever I rested it against the wall, but no magic throbbed in my veins. *Would it happen with time, or were the stories just that, stories? Had Adelaide's assumptions about the Fairshaw Master's magic been wrong?*

I met with groups of scholars, and upper class callers left their cards with Stonier all morning. The hours of visiting were long and tiresome. I never knew toffs were so busy, but thanked the saints *I* was. *My tight schedule made it easy to push away the disgust in Adelaide's eyes as she'd called me a murderer.*

But while my days left no time to ponder what she might be up to—night was a different beast to be dealt with. I assumed she slept in our bed, so I spent my nights in a bedchamber on a separate floor. But rather than sleeping, my mind spun with thoughts of her. I longed for the woman who'd snuck out to a hop vine to get away from the stilted life unsuited to her adventurous spirit. I missed her laugh in the dark, wrapping around me like velvet. Missed the shade of white her hair turned under the moonlight. *Where was the woman who'd defied convention to search me out on Pendle Street, who'd thrown her gloves to the floor, and held no part of herself back as she'd kissed me?*

When I finally laid eyes on my wife again, three miserable days had passed since our wedding, and her skin lacked the rosiness I remembered. The dark circles under her glassy eyes caused a stab of guilt. *Was she still sick? Torn up by my leaving?* Part of me felt vindicated that she'd suffered as much as I did. *If my nights were to be spent sleepless, hers should be too.*

I hadn't killed for her, and she ought to know me well enough to assume as much. But she'd labeled me a murderer without waiting to hear my defense. After everything we'd shared—hearts more than bodies—it felt like the deepest betrayal.

I watched Adelaide's fingers trail over the stack of books on the table by the door where she stood. She flicked one of them open and bent her head as she followed the lines of letters. Letting out a sigh that tugged on my heartstrings, she closed the book and straightened. As if she sensed me, her head lifted, and she stopped in her tracks. Holding her shuttered gaze from across the room was a far cry from the intimacy we'd known before our wedding. If I'd known this would be the outcome, would I have hunted the cat with as much fervor that day when I thought all was lost? *Yes, you would have. Because you love her.*

I sighed. I was the Fairshaw Master, with a library full of magic and the knowledge of every book in the world, but it eluded me why love must be such a wretched feeling.

Adelaide held my stare for a long moment, then she

whirled and ran from the room. But not before I saw the shine of tears threatening to spill. The pain in her eyes was another punch to my gut. How did she make me feel so guilty? *She was the one who was at fault for this, damn it! Stupid self-righteous, wretched...wife.*

I cursed her name under my breath as I stormed after her. The heavy oak door of our bedchamber slammed shut as I reached it, damn near taking my fingertips with it in the process. I swore. Probably louder than I should have. Reining in my anger, I tried to reason with my hurt pride. She might be at fault, but shouldn't I be the bigger man? The muffled sobs I heard through the door suggested as much.

Pride fought a battle with my conscience. *I ought to comfort her, force her to listen until she knew the truth.* My conscience twitched as sobs turned to quiet hiccups on the other side of the oak panel. But she'd called me a murderer, evaded my touch, and eyed my hands as if they were the limbs of a monster. Again, I recalled the disgust in her eyes when I'd tried to pull her close. The way she'd shrunk away.

Anger rose again.

And pride won.

CHAPTER 30

Adelaide

I held my breath and listened for footsteps. Nothing. Lowering my shoulders, I drew in a breath of air saturated with mystery and wood polish. Then turned the corner to the west wing.

I moved like a fugitive in a strange place—not the way the Fairshaw's daughter should be moving through the building where she'd lived all her life. *Except, my title was no longer that of daughter. I was the Fairshaw's wife. A murderer's wife.*

I came upon another open doorway and slowed my steps. When I heard no voices within, I hurried past it. I hadn't spoken to Frederick in the four days since he'd left our room in anger, and I didn't want to now. My heart ached that the man I was finally free to love had let greed make such a terrifying choice for him. He'd followed me to my room yesterday, but I didn't want to hear his excuses, or his justifications. *What if my love for him made me see past his cruelty? What if I forgave him?* Both scenarios terrified me. And worse yet, he was the Fairshaw Master. What did that mean for the future of the town I loved?

I halted my steps and leaned against the wall for support. I'd never felt so weak in my life. Was my turmoil about the man I loved wearing on me? Illness couldn't harm Fairshaws, but could heartache? Nausea roiled in my stomach and my head felt buoyant. Fighting another wave of dizziness, I pushed away from the wall.

Why did he have to be so wonderful? Why had he let me see how much he cared for his sisters, and why had he saved me—both from the drunkards in the woods and from falling to my death?

It would have been so much easier to let him go if he hadn't kissed me as if I was all he wanted from life. If I hadn't known that his touch could light my skin on fire. If I could forget the way his eyes lit with mischief and darkened with desire.

I was about to turn the corner to the west wing, when Frederick's deep voice sounded from the doorway. I turned quickly and hurried down the hall, hoping the rustle of my skirts wouldn't alert him. But that same rumbling bass followed me, and unease skittered over my skin. Desperate to escape, I pressed down on the nearest door handle, and slipped inside the room.

Closing the door quietly, I turned to see medical journals lining the walls. Years ago, this had been my father's study. *In my memories, I could barely see over the armrest of the wingback chair by the fireplace. I remembered the burning heat of the flames against my cheeks and his stern voice from the chair, telling my nurse to return me to my room.*

Stepping over the intricately patterned carpet, I let my fingers slip over the smooth wooden top of the chair where he'd sat. I didn't miss him. But I did miss the father I could have had. *The one who'd have wanted me.*

Before my marriage, I would have tugged a book from the shelves and curled up in this chair to read. Elizabeth would have lit the fire, and I'd have spent blissful hours devouring the written word in the cozy room. My soul had known perfect happiness sampling the faraway worlds and thrilling ideas saved in the tomes all around me. I'd never felt trapped in this mansion of endless rooms, high ceilings, and ample magic—I would never have thought it possible.

But now I did.

I'd never thought I could be lonely in the company of my books. But as I considered the endless years looming before me, ones spent married to a murderer, the cold feeling echoed through my bones. Any other woman could have asked for a divorce, and I would have gladly faced the scorn of high society, but Fairshaw marriages could only be dissolved by death. *And, miserable as I was, I still wanted to live.*

I crossed to the window overlooking the numerous labyrinths of fragrant herbs, exotic fruits, and flowers whose names even I would need to look up. I knew every corner of that garden by heart. When had I last walked it? Before my wedding it had been daily. Now I didn't want Frederick to corner me there. *No, the inside of the Library was safer.*

Pulling a small volume from the shelf closest to the window, I flipped through the pages. My eyes scanned the letters, but no magic sparkled off the page. Ever since I'd promised my life to Frederick, the written word had refused to connect with my soul. Was I no longer connected to my magic? *Had my husband's choice to murder for the Fairshaw title somehow altered the magic itself?*

Male heirs kept their powers their whole lives, but I was the first female heir in centuries. Was it the same for me? Or had I lost it during our vows? For a moment, I almost wished my father was here to guide me. If I truly was detached from my magic, the sickness that had taken over my body would make sense.

Overwhelming fatigue had chained me to my bed the first day of our marriage, and even now that I was back on my feet, each movement was a struggle as I pushed through the nausea. Worst was the pain. It burned across my ribs, restricting my airflow and numbing my left side as if I'd received a mortal wound there. Just yesterday, the intense sensation had made me remove my clothes to search in vain for cuts and bruises to explain the pressure.

Another wave hit, and I gripped the window sill so tightly my knuckles turned white. Breathing deeply through my nose, I closed my eyes and pressed my lips together against the piercing pain.

"Adelaide?" Frederick's voice startled me. *How had I not heard him enter the room?* The heavy breaths that filled the air answered my question. Another searing pain hit, and I groaned loudly. *I couldn't take it anymore. Not the pain, not this marriage, not him.*

Oh, the irony. Thinking my judgment of him had been too hasty, I'd fallen in love with the leering opportunist who'd climbed up to my window, only to find that he really was a worse villain than I'd first accused him of. *Suddenly it all seemed hilarious.*

A hollow smile flitted across my face—I was losing my sanity, just like I'd lost my good judgment. "Adelaide what's wrong with you? Why are you smiling?"

Frederick's wife smiled at him and it turned the concern in his voice to fear. The laugh that escaped on my next breath sounded wrong. *Did I not smile enough? I definitely didn't smile enough.*

"Are you drunk?" *Oh, if only.* I giggled and took an unsteady step away from the window. The world spun with my movement. Frederick's arms closed around my body. Then, glorious numbness stole over me, and the darkness pulled me in.

CHAPTER 31

Adelaide

Searing flames licked my skin. I tried to roll over, away from the fire, but couldn't. *Was I paralyzed?* I had to be paralyzed. Terror clamped over my ribs, and a terrified whimper stole out through my parched lips.

"Shh, don't move." Frederick's whisper sounded in my ear. His voice was warm, concerned, like the time on the hop vine when he'd tucked me close to him to keep my teeth from chattering. *But that was so long ago, wasn't it?* Why was he here now? The frown digging between my brows sent white-hot pain through my skull.

Immediately, I relaxed my facial muscles. Frederick's chest rose and fell against my back, and understanding clawed its way through my muddled brain. *His arms were the reason I couldn't move.* Relief crashed through me. "Why are you here?" My voice was a croak.

"You've been really sick." None of the self-assurance I associated with him was in his voice, only a thread of…fear? The same fear I'd heard when he'd found me in my father's old study? But what did this man have to be fearful of? He was the Fairshaw Master, and however undeserved, the powers that used to be my father's were his.

I tried to pull the moments before I fainted out of the dark abyss of my memories. I'd been laughing. Because of the fear in Frederick's voice? But that couldn't be right. "Was I out long?"

"Six days."

I chuckled, but he did not. Fear gripped me as he ran his hand lightly along my arm. "Don't talk too much, I don't want you to exert yourself." The forced calm in his voice told me more than his words ever could. *He really was afraid.*

I attempted to move, but his arms didn't yield. "Let me turn." He loosened his hold, but my own movements still felt as if I was working against iron chains. I snuggled my face against his shirt, breathing in the scent that was all Frederick. His heart beat steadily under my ear, calming me, renewing my strength.

I loved him.

It didn't matter that I didn't like him, that I didn't want to. I should be disgusted with myself for loving a killer. Silent tears slipped down my face at the thought, soaking the soft linen under my cheek.

His breath warmed the top of my head, and wrapped in my own misery, it took me a second to realize he was talking, his voice muffled against my hair. "Why are you crying? Are you in pain?"

I pressed closer to him, and calm settled in my chest. I could finally breathe for the first time in a long time. Since our wedding? Before that?

"I wanted you, Frederick. I've missed you so much. I…" The words stuck in my throat, and I couldn't continue.

He exhaled against my hair. "I was here the whole time." There was no accusation in his words, but he was right. *I* had pushed *him* away, not the other way around.

Even so. "I can't apologize."

"Why is that?" My jaw tightened around the words I wanted to speak. I didn't want to argue with him. Not when he was holding me for the first time in weeks. I wanted to be tucked up against his heart like this forever, for his touches to stay reverent like this. Wanted him to keep holding me as if I was everything to him. How could I tell him what I really thought of him without pushing him away? "Adelaide, are you still with me? Did you fall asleep?"

"No." But I couldn't let him speak. I didn't trust myself not to forgive him. Memories of the man who'd twirled his sister around my bedroom surfaced. *The joy in his smile as he gazed down at her wispy curls framing her face.* Did I still believe the sincerity in his voice as he'd tried to put my fears to rest?

"I just want to be allowed to say no."

"And for what it's worth, Miss Fairshaw, when I'm your husband, that will be your right.

Frederick rubbed his hand between my shoulder blades, and I melted into him with a sigh. "You're not sorry for pushing me away?"

I tried to ignore the hurt in his voice, even as I looked up to find tenderness in his eyes. I lowered my gaze, refusing to hold his for longer than a second. That second was more than enough to make me struggle to hold onto my defenses. "You killed someone to get the key. How could I let you touch me after that?" A moot point, as the very hand that had spilled that blood presently played with my hair while his other rubbed the ache from my shoulders.

His body stiffened underneath my cheek and he let out a hard breath. "I didn't." How could he lie with such sincerity? It made me doubt everything I thought I knew about him. Fear pulsed through my veins. I tried to pull away, but his arms stayed around me, and I was too weak to fight them. "Stay with me Adelaide. Give me a chance to tell you the truth."

I stared daggers into his chest, refusing to give him my eyes.

"When I came to you and the Library was closed, I panicked." He paused, tucked a strand of blonde away from my face and pressed a soft kiss to my forehead. My heart wavered, but I forced myself to hold my closed off expression. "I can't promise that I wouldn't have done whatever necessary to get my hands on the key. But I didn't have to face that choice."

How had he not? Was this another one of his lies? I held my breath for his next words. "The cat was dead when I found it."

Grief pushed through the pores of my skin like toxic smoke, and the sharp, numbing ache settled in my chest. I sobbed into his shirt, and he folded me ever so gently against him. "What kind of monster would kill a magical, innocent creature?"

He shook his head, pressed warm lips to my temple. "I don't know. Wild animals?"

Anger rose in my chest. "No."

The cat was as much a part of the Library magic as I was. Why hadn't I felt it die? "It couldn't have been. Wild animals wouldn't be able to kill a magical cat!"

"What then? What man would kill the animal that

could bring him the Fairshaw Library?" *Who, indeed?*

But another thought pushed its way through my grief-struck mind. One that mattered more than the numbing loss of the cat. I grasped for it, and as the realization took hold, my eyes widened. "Where did you get the key, then?"

"It was still on its collar when I found it."

I pulled in a sharp breath. *Was he lying? Or had he told the truth the whole time?* Finally daring to look up, I held his dark gaze, searching for a glimmer of greed in the depths of his eyes. Where was the calculating gleam I'd seen the day we met?

He held my gaze. Not backing down from my challenge, not shuttering his emotions like I'd seen him do so often. His dark eyes were honest, if brimming with pain.

Had I put that pain there by refusing to hear him out? By pouncing on the first opportunity I'd had to doubt him? But how could I not have?

I'd seen the greed in his eyes that day he'd climbed up to my window. Heard his indifferent words by the ruins in the woods. Felt the warmth leave his smile as he'd promised to do anything to get his hands on the key. *Was he like his sister had said, both the honorable brother and the wicked opportunist?*

He leaned forward and rested his forehead against mine. "I didn't kill anyone, Adelaide. Please believe me."

I waited for the warning bells in my mind to go off. Waited for the assurance deep in my soul that he was feeding me another pretty lie. But none came. Instead, I felt the truth of his words deep down into my bones. *He was telling the truth.*

Relief gushed through my chest. *I wasn't burning up with love for a murderer.* Then remorse clutched my lungs. *What had I put him through by accusing him like this?* I pressed my palm to his stubbled cheek, and he leaned into it. "Frederick. I'm so sorry."

Hope flickered in his eyes, and I hated the uncertainty I saw there. How much time had we lost from my determination not to believe him? Regret squeezed my chest again, and words spilled over my lips like a waterfall. "I should have listened to you. I'm so terribly sorry I didn't listen to you." I pulled him to me, needing him to feel my apology.

He stayed unyielding, for a moment that seemed to last years—

Then his mouth crashed against mine. Magic pounded, sparkled through my veins. His warm breath and solid heat everything I'd missed while we'd been apart.

My fingers tunneled through his dark hair, tugging at the strands. I scraped my nails along his scalp, and his groan made me laugh—the sound drowned in another kiss. A magical, glittering kiss that sent energy skittering across my skin, that—

"Wait." The word was a rusty groan, drawn out as he pulled away with effort—as if his body was held against mine by magic. "Adelaide. You've been so sick. My magic is supposed to heal you, but it's been taking too long. We shouldn't…"

I reached for him, and his eyes flared with heat, but he held his ground.

I shook my head. "We should."

A war between desire and concern filled his eyes. "You almost died. I thought you were dying." His voice broke, and my heart bled for him. Wrapping my fingers around his calloused hand, I pressed it against my chest. My pounding heart picked up speed as the pain retreated from his eyes, replaced by embers of desire.

Mouth dry under the intensity of his stare, I wet my lips. His eyes followed the movement, and those embers fanned into flame. I swallowed, my heart hammering my ribs and his hand. "Does this feel like death to you?"

Hunger flared in his eyes, and his mouth moved to mine. "No." Brushed mine. "Like life." Devoured mine.

CHAPTER 32

Frederick

I held her against me long after she fell asleep—the feel of her bare skin against mine its own kind of magic.

We'd wasted so much time. If I'd been forthcoming with her from the start this could have been just another night of our shared life. Sure, she'd refused to listen to reason, but couldn't I have swallowed my pride and yelled the truth through the door she'd slammed in my face? If she'd never gotten sick, would we have spent our lives avoiding each other?

Her illness had mystified her late father's doctor. She shouldn't have fallen ill in the first place but still should have healed from my magic. Concluding our separate lives were to blame and my new magic simply too weak to heal her from afar, he'd insisted on our current arrangement. I hadn't wanted to hold her, knowing her reaction to my touch when conscious—worry about her health was the only reason I'd consented. And she'd still tossed and turned with feverish dreams for six days and six nights.

The memory of her pained whimpers… I shuddered and tightened my arms around her. Breathed in her sweet scent, and pressed a kiss to her warm forehead. *Too warm.*

Alarm bells clanged through my mind. Her skin was too hot against my mouth. *Had she not turned a corner with her illness when she woke up this evening?* I ran my hand down her arm, squeezed her fingers, and found the flesh there just as heated. *All of her was burning up!* I pushed the covers off of us, hoping the chilled night air would cool her.

"Adelaide?" Her eyes were closed, and she could have been asleep if not for her ghastly pale face. I repeated her name again and again without response, my voice thin with fear in the quiet room. Frantic, I slid my fingers along the underside of her jaw, finally locating a faint pulse. I swore, then yelled at the top of my lungs.

The door burst open as Adelaide's maid ran into the room, lamp in hand. Her eyes went wide as she took in the scene before her. "I need you to get the doctor. Immediately." My voice brooked no contest.

The maid nodded and curtsied. "Yes, Master Fairshaw."

Minutes later she returned with the old man who'd watched over my wife since she'd fainted in my arms a week ago. Remembering her state of undress, I moved the sheet up to her chin. I found my shirt on the floor and pulled it on, tugging the fabric over my own bare hips. The doctor leaned over Adelaide, touched his fingers to her jaw and bent to listen to her shallow breathing.

I shoved a hand through my hair, needing desperately to help and having no idea what I could do. *Wasn't the Fairshaw Master supposed to have all knowledge and power? Where was mine?* Not only could I not heal my wife—I didn't know what to do to help her. Was this what Adelaide's father had gone through when her mother had—no. I wasn't going there.

My wife was going to live.

The doctor's grave eyes met mine. "How long has she been unresponsive?"

My hands fisted at my sides. "She seemed fine before she fell asleep, but her fever returned, and I can't get her to answer me."

He murmured something to himself, and fear got in another jab to my gut. "Sir, I need you to leave." His demand was as stern as my reply.

"I'll be staying." He could try to make me, but I wasn't leaving her. *Not now that I knew she loved me.*

The doctor sighed, then shifted his attention to his patient. He lowered the sheet and ran his fingers along her neck. "Miss Masfield? Help me get her to a seated position." The maid supported her mistress in an upright position and the doctor pressed his head to Adelaide's back. He shook his head and they lowered her. The doctor slapped Adelaide's cheek, and I roared. He straightened. "Master Fairshaw, I cannot treat your wife with you in the room. You're impeding her treatment by staying."

I drilled my eyes into her maid, who somehow took no offense. "I will keep her safe, Master Fairshaw. I promise."

I nodded and left the room to pace the hallway outside it. Days seemed to pass before the maid peeked out, and I almost smacked her with the heavy oak door in my eagerness to get back inside. I rushed to Adelaide's side and knelt by the head of the bed. Resting my forehead against hers, I laced our fingers together. *Thank God hers were cooler now.*

The doctor spoke behind me, but I couldn't take my eyes off of her beautiful face. "Her fever is gone, but she's weak. Don't let her talk too much."

"You scared me." I whispered the words against her hair. She croaked my name, and the sound was heavenly. "Shh, you don't need to talk, love." I kissed her temple.

She cleared her throat. "Frederick, I think my life is

208

linked to—" A violent cough racked her body, and she whimpered. The sound of her pain made me want to actually kill something. She gasped. "The cat—"

"Your life can't be linked to the Fairshaw Cat. It's dead." The pain in her eyes squeezed my insides, and panic clamped onto my lungs. "You're not dying." She couldn't die. *She wasn't going to die.* "When did you first feel sick?"

Another coughing fit muffled her answer, and she tried again. "When the doors locked."

The Fairshaw Cat had still been warm when I'd found it. Again I saw her as I had that day, through the glass, slumped against her bedchamber door. *If she'd gotten sick as it had received its mortal wound, what were the chances it was a coincidence?*

Adelaide gestured to the glass of water on her bedside table. I picked it up and held it to her mouth, one arm supporting her back. She swallowed a sip, then pressed her lips together and sank back against my arm as if the little effort had tired her out.

"You didn't tell me you were sick." The words sounded like an accusation, and perhaps they were. *Why hadn't she told me?*

"I thought it was just lack of sleep from worrying, and we didn't talk until after the wedding." *Of course she would have thought that.* For all she knew, the fears she'd shared with me in the days before the wedding had come true. When the doors closed and I showed up without the key, she would have thought she was marrying a stranger. Despair kicked its way through my defenses. I'd failed her. *But how could I have protected her against this?*

"And *after* the wedding?" I ground the words out as if they had the power to break my teeth.

Another cough. "I kept getting sicker." I gently lowered her back to the pillows. If she was right that her life was linked to the Fairshaw Cat's, it was only a matter of time before…

I shoved my fists against my eyes and rose to my feet. No. It couldn't end like this. I wasn't going to watch my wife fade away in front of me. Bands of steel weighed down my heart, cutting fresh wounds into the flesh there.

I'd seen a woman as strong and full of life as Adelaide succumb to death before. My mother's face still came to me in my dreams—void of life in my nightmares. A sound from Adelaide had me on my knees by her side again. "What?"

Her eyes, dark blue depths of pain and regret, slayed me. "I love you." It wasn't a declaration of love—*these were last words.*

"No! You're not saying goodbye to me. I'll find a way to fight this!" I framed her beautiful face and kissed her mouth, too cool against mine. Fear slithered and spun its way through my chest. "Promise me you won't give up." The faint murmur against my mouth was impossible to decipher, and still I pulled back. "I'm coming back for you."

I strode for the Library entrance without waiting for a reply. I'd slit my own throat if it would heal her, and this would hurt as badly. *But not as much as watching her die, knowing I could have saved her.*

Chapter 33

Frederick

Gasping for breath after my run, I reached the steps of the stately town home. The master of this estate was no friend of mine, though for the woman I'd left gliding the line between life and death at the Library, I'd do anything. *Including striking a bargain with Dr. Harrison.*

I propped my hands on my thighs as I struggled to draw air, but Adelaide's shining eyes in my mind's eye gave me energy I didn't know I had. I ran up the stone steps to the entrance, burst through the door without knock or greeting, ignoring the butler's silver tray as well as his protests.

"I need to see Dr. Harrison. It's urgent."

"But Sir, it's barely past breakfast."

I blinked while my eyes adjusted to the interior of the house, dark compared to the morning light outside.

"Master Fairshaw. What can I do for you?" My knees nearly buckled with relief as I made out the man entering the room. My chest heaved, and the words stuck in my throat. My successor brushed a powdery residue off his hands. "I wouldn't have expected the Fairshaw to venture out and about so soon after his wedding. Shouldn't you be...enjoying...your new circumstances?" His smooth voice revealed nothing of his devious mind, but my opinion of this man didn't matter. His skill for healing was unsurpassed, and that was the quality I needed.

His dark eyes surveyed me in question, but I knew he must already be aware of Adelaide's illness. Gossip traveled fast through town, and Adelaide was much better liked than her father had been. Not to mention, tongues had already been wagging about our wedding. Probably our separate sleeping quarters, too. *I'd quickly learned the downside to having servants.*

I wanted to leave this cursed place and the presence of this vile man, but Adelaide needed me to make this bargain. "I need your help." The words scratched my throat raw.

He bowed, glittering eyes never leaving mine. "I'm at your service, Fairshaw."

I thought of the tears in Martha's eyes as I'd handed her the purse of coins the day after my wedding. Would it be enough for her to live on from now on?

Liv's face swam before my eyes, her cheeks rounder since I'd married Adelaide. I'd failed my sisters again, and the guilt cut deep. I cleared my throat. "My wife is dying.

Something killed the Fairshaw Cat, and because their lives were linked she's also dying."

Surprise crossed his features. "I didn't think the magical Fairshaw Cat could be killed? And who would do it?"

Who indeed? I raked my hand over my face, barely able to shut Adelaide's pale countenance out long enough to truly see the man in front of me. Terror pressed down on my lungs, making it difficult to breathe, much less think clearly.

"Sacrifice." I forced the rest of the words out of my mouth before I could change my mind. "Sacrifice thwarts death."

Dr. Harrison's eyes glinted darkly, and he took a step closer towards me. "So it's true what they say—that the Fairshaw Master inhabits the knowledge of the great Library."

I ignored his jab at my limited schooling. I had little respect for this man and expected none in return. I was here for what he had that I lacked. I stepped forward, my boots barely lifting off the polished floor. As if I was the one dying, not the wife I'd left behind. "I need you to accept my position as Fairshaw."

His shrewd eyes narrowed and greed glinted in his eyes. *I'd known that greed once, and it had almost cost me the woman I loved.* "Why me, Fairshaw?"

"If my sacrifice doesn't heal her completely, you will have the knowledge needed to help her recover."

"And in return you require what?"

My words croaked through my parched throat. "Nothing. I can't, or the sacrifice might not be great enough." I wasn't above begging. "Please heal her. I need her to live."

Dr. Harrison looked stunned for a moment, and when he spoke, his voice was filled with surprise. "You would really give up your position as Fairshaw, and your claim to your wife?"

"For her life, yes." There was no doubt. I would give anything for Adelaide's life, even the opportunity to live out my days by her side.

"When?"

Adelaide had no time to lose. She could already be… No. I needed my focus to be here, with Dr. Harrison, *so she could live.* My voice was steady, but the hand I held out to him shook. "Now."

Dr. Harrison's smooth, pale hand curled around mine. I cleared my throat and tightened my fingers around his. "I pass to you all my powers as Fairshaw, all knowledge and riches of the Fairshaw Library, and my marriage vows to Adelaide Fairshaw."

As soon as I spoke the words, prickling heat burned in the center of my palm and spread out through my fingers.

Magic like I'd never felt when I was the Fairshaw spread through my fingers, my arm. A force like a strong wind wrapped around our hands, pressing them together. Pain tore through my hand and wrist, lasting only a moment— then the tingling stopped and my hand immediately cooled, as if I'd submerged it in ice water. I retrieved my hand from Dr. Harrison's as blood slowly returned to warm it. I turned it in front of my face, flexing my fingers, but no marks matched the burning pain of seconds ago. *It was done.*

Across from me, Dr. Harrison studied his hand like I had. I tugged on the silver key I carried around my neck, tore the chain, and handed it to him. "Go. If it didn't work, she has little time to lose." I stared him down, as if my gaze could set him in motion. *Perhaps, if I hadn't given up my powers, it could have.*

He nodded, pocketed the key, grabbed his coat from the butler, and walked through the door I'd never shut. I expected him to walk on, but he stopped on the other side of the threshold with an expectant expression. "I'd like you to leave my house, Holloway."

Holloway. No longer a Fairshaw. I had my old name back, my old life. Pain seared through me at the thought of what I'd willingly given up. Dr. Harrison cleared his throat.

I was wasting moments Adelaide might need. I walked through the door and watched as he paused to shrug his coat over his shoulders, each second he didn't go to her aid, agony. "Please, go to her."

"I will do it, Holloway." Dr. Harrison tucked the key into his inner pocket and walked with hurried steps across the same cobblestones my feet had pounded minutes ago. He turned the corner, and my legs gave out. The wet ground dampened my trousers, chilling me as I waited for the strength to stand. *Would I ever find it without her by my side?*

I hadn't spared a thought for this woman when I'd made my decision to find the Fairshaw Cat. How had she come to change the direction of my life? How had loving her made me give up the opportunity of a lifetime?

But as my breath returned to normal and the stitch in my side eased, I knew hunting for the Fairshaw Cat had changed me. Because as I sat here, fine trousers soaked through and hair wild from running my fingers through it, looking not at all like the gentleman I'd been when I'd left her, I knew without a doubt.

I'd do it all again—for her.

Chapter 34

Adelaide

A cool hand settled on my brow, and a chilled glass touched my lips. Sweet liquid met my tongue, and I drank deeply of the nectar held to my mouth. "That's a good girl."

Startled by the unfamiliar voice, my eyes sprang open to reveal a pale face bent over me. Another doctor? "Who are you?"

The space between his dark brows narrowed. "Dr. Ralph Harrison…Fairshaw."

I gasped as my mind filled with the memories of the man who had struck the little boy. Who'd spoken so cruelly about those less fortunate than him. His eyes hadn't stopped taking me in since I'd woken up. What had those eyes seen while I'd slept? I shuddered.

Then my mind caught on the name he'd given me, and my breath stuck in my throat. *Harrison Fairshaw.* But Dr.

Harrison wasn't the Fairshaw. He couldn't be? If he was, then Frederick must have…

Pain seared through me and a wail rose in my throat. "No!" The sweet liquid I'd swallowed so greedily dribbled out the sides of my mouth as I wept for the man I loved.

"Lady Fairshaw." Dr. Harrison put his hand on my shoulder, and I recoiled in disgust.

"You killed him." I spat curses at him. "You evil—"

"Mr. Holloway isn't dead, Lady Fairshaw."

Men killed for the Fairshaw title, as I'd thought Frederick had. And Dr. Harrison was the furthest thing from a saint. I didn't believe for a second he hadn't hurt him. Tears streamed down my cheeks. "If my husband is still alive, how come you have his name? The title of Fairshaw can only be transferred by succession or marriage."

"He surrendered his title to me."

The salty taste of tears slipped into the corners of my mouth. Frederick loved me! He would never have given up his title, or our marriage, willingly. "That's not possible. If it was, I would have heard of it."

"You've never heard of anyone surrendering the Fairshaw title because most men would rather die fighting to keep it than to give it away, not because surrendering it is impossible."

The Frederick I knew would have sacrificed anything to keep his title as Fairshaw. Nothing could have persuaded him to give it up. No riches surpassed those of the Library—the power and magic held by the Fairshaw was unmatched. There simply wasn't anything better to trade it for. I scoffed. "Are you trying to tell me that my husband gave up his title? He would never do that."

He watched me with an unnerving calm. "But Mr. Holloway found something he cared for more than the Fairshaw Library's riches."

"What could possibly mean more to him than the Fairshaw Library?" *More than me?*

"Your life."

I blinked, and my last memory came flooding back. Cold had traveled through my limbs, and fog had resided at the edges of my consciousness. I'd slurred my declaration of love, and Frederick had ordered me not to give up—*I had been dying.* "But Frederick found the key after the cat died, how did his giving it up change anything?"

The man in front of me leaned back. "Mr. Holloway found the key *after* the cat was killed? *So the transfer was not complete.*" The last part was barely a mumble, as if he'd meant the words only for himself.

"But the doors opened for him when he had the key, so it must have been complete!"

Dr. Harrison made a sound of derision. "If your former husband had been the true heir, he would have died soon after, from the wounds inflicted on the cat. They should have transferred to him, not you."

Cold fear writhed in my belly. I closed my eyes to push away the image of Frederick's lifeless eyes staring back at me, but the visions in my mind were worse. *So much worse.*

My eyes sprang open to find Dr. Harrison's shrewd gaze on me. I saw not a hint of compassion there. "Are you saying that Frederick is dying instead of me?"

"No."

I felt sick. "Then what? I don't understand!"

"The antidote to death is sacrifice. Your former husband sacrificed what he loved most, his life with you, and because of that sacrifice your invisible wounds healed. I am your husband now—for the moment."

I didn't trust the man in front of me any more than I had before, but his words rang true. Which begged another question. *If Frederick was alive, where was he?*

Dr. Harrison held the cup out again. "You need to drink the rest of this."

I pulled back. "What does it do? I thought you said Frederick's sacrifice healed me?"

He shook his head. "You're fully healed, but your body is weak."

I hesitated. *Would Frederick have left my care to this man if he hadn't trusted his healing skills?* I leaned forward, took the cup, and let the sweet liquid spill down my throat. The temperature in the room dropped by several degrees, and I shivered as I emptied the cup and licked my lips. Dr. Harrison's eyes followed the movement, and I set my jaw.

He refilled the cup from a small bottle and offered it again. This drink burned my lips, and I choked down the first sip. Desperate to distract myself from the horrid taste, I asked the question that had been swirling in my mind for the last few minutes. "What did you mean by 'married at the moment'? Aren't Fairshaw marriages life-long?"

He laughed, but the sound held no joy. "Seeing as you were married to Mr. Holloway and aren't anymore, hardly. I mean to divorce you once you regain your strength."

I tipped the cup again and pushed away the affront his words inspired—I didn't want to be married to this man, and the less time we spent as husband and wife, the better. But why a divorce? Unless... My throat burned from the rising bile. "Wouldn't an annulment be sufficient?"

His eyes glittered, as if my discomfort was enjoyable to him. "An annulment means the marriage never happened and would leave me no longer the Fairshaw. So although we were never married in the physical sense, our marriage needs to have happened and be broken. That way I will be heir to Fairshaw, and you will be free to marry Mr. Holloway if you so wish."

I let out the breath I'd been holding. My heart felt light at the thought of being Frederick's wife again. I desperately missed his touch, his voice. The calm that wrapped around my soul whenever he was near. But if Frederick still wanted me, why wasn't he here? Had he given up the Fairshaw title to wash his hands of me? *After all I'd put him through, it would be more than fair.*

But we'd made up, hadn't we? Or had I dreamed that? I pulled the covers up to my chin as I gazed around the room we'd barely shared. "You don't know where Frederick is?"

"I'm not your former husband's keeper, am I?" Annoyance slipped into Dr. Harrison's voice.

He wasn't the only one. My nostrils flared. "Why are you even here?"

His eyes narrowed. "I'm your husband and a renowned doctor. My wife was on her deathbed, and my presence was expected."

"Well, she's fine now, so you're welcome to leave." I drained the glass and shoved it into his hand. The movement made the room spin as if I was falling backwards, despite the sturdy support of pillows behind me. I tried to scowl at the man in front of me, but his pale face

223

swam in and out of focus. "What is this drink?"

My eyelids lowered as if weighed down by a thousand weights, and my leaden hand sank to the mattress. I drifted away from consciousness to the sound of his answer.

"Sleeping draught."

CHAPTER 35

Frederick

Laughter rang through the hazy air of Rupert's pub as the curly-haired girl seated on Billy Davis's lap told another joke. A burly man with a silver streaked beard slapped his meaty hands on his thighs and roared with laughter. "Did you hear that one, Holloway?"

I rolled my eyes. One had to be at least half scammered to think her quip was remotely funny, and I hadn't had much more than a sip of the drink in front of me. Billy Davis gave the girl a kiss, and whistles and lewd comments mingled with an off-tune violin. I was surprised she didn't recoil just from being near him.

The man who'd first addressed me leaned closer. "Ey, Holloway, you don't think she's funny? Bit o' raspberry like her?"

I glanced at the girl in question. She was pretty enough, but she was no Adelaide Fairshaw. Hollow pain clanged against the bars of my ribs. *Adelaide. My wife.*

No, not mine.

Dr. Harrison's wife. My stomach roiled.

A lanky boy I'd watched grow up stumbled closer and slammed his hand down on the man's shoulder. "Don't try to cheer him up, mate. He's lost all his humor since he moved out of the Library. There's..." He hiccoughed, waving his other hand in my direction. "There's nothing... He's no fun anymore."

Bloody right I wasn't.

A gasp sounded from behind me, and a hand clamped onto my shoulder. This man's breath reeked of stale ale. "Mate! You moved out of the Fairshaw Library? Now why would you do that?" Not about to answer that, I shrugged his hand off.

My old neighbor chimed in. "You must be new to town, ey? Well, you see, Holloway here—"

I didn't care to hear another fabricated story of my fall from grace or speculations about why I no longer held the Fairshaw title. Not one of the rumors I'd heard had been close to the truth, but that didn't mean I had any interest in listening in. I rose so abruptly from the table my chair tumbled to the floor behind me. Angry shouts rose from the several men whose drinks I had spilled. Curses followed me as I stepped over my chair.

"Good riddance Holloway!"

I pushed my way through the crowd as whiffs of alcohol and unwashed bodies slammed against my senses. Slender fingers clamped onto my coat in passing, and a silky voice sounded in my ear. "Sir, don't leave yet…"

Shrugging the girl off, I escaped into the night before she found the courage to try again. I stepped over a small bundle crouched up against the doorpost outside Rupert's. Light snores came from the rags. A child?

Pity squirmed in my chest, but I wanted out of this place. And what could I do anyways? *I wasn't the Fairshaw Master anymore. My wages weren't enough to support even my own sisters.*

I stepped away, leaving the child to sleep, the sound of my boots against cobblestone loud in the quiet alley. I strode on down Abbey Street. It was late enough for proper townsfolk to be asleep, but the inhabitants of this place weren't that. Two of them were seconds away from turning their heated discussion into a fistfight. I gave them a wide berth and ignored the shouts coming from the dilapidated building behind them. The urine stench of the cobblestones made my eyes water. And still, I should be used to it, shouldn't I? Had my scant two weeks as a proper gentleman ruined me for the life I'd been born into?

I turned the corner and up another street, this one near deserted. Except for the trio of women weaving towards me, arms slung around each other's waists.

"Are you lonely tonight, good sir?" The woman's hoarse voice grated, and her clear offer made bile rise in my throat. I ignored her bold gaze and walked past, hands stuffed deep in my pockets.

Shuffling sounded behind me, then a chorus of giggles. "Molly! That's Frederick Holloway!"

An exaggerated gasp sounded, and then the first woman's voice again. "Sorry, Fairshaw, no offense!" Their peals of laughter echoed between the houses.

Had I really thought there'd be any obscurity to sink back into for the Holloway who'd pretended to be a gentleman? Had another man been in my shoes, wouldn't I have regarded him with the same derision? *Probably.*

The further I got from the docks, the sweeter the scent of the cobblestones. A horse neighed somewhere nearby. A lone chimney sweep, still in his work garb, knelt in the gutter, mumbling quietly to himself in between bouts of vomiting. Somewhere nearby a tomcat regaled sleeping townspeople with his music. A creaking window opened, and curses flew out into the night.

Of their own volition, my steps had brought me to the looming iron gates of the Fairshaw Library. I lifted my gaze to the brick manor that towered over the town below it. *My home for a short while.*

The clock tower chimed behind me as midnight settled over the Fairshaw, and my eyes trailed the climbing vine that wound its way from the ground to the rooftop. Clusters of hop leaves circled darkened windows, and somewhere within those walls slept the woman I loved. My wife.

I'd neither heard nor seen her in the weeks since I'd surrendered my title. A fortnight had come and gone—the longest one of my life. When I'd called at the Library to inquire about her health. Stonier had turned me away every time, delivering the same message with unease in his eyes. *"Lady Fairshaw is resting and wants no visitors."*

My only news of her health were secondhand, through Martha's conversations with Adelaide's lady's maid. According to them, Adelaide was healing. It didn't change the fact that I woke up in a cold sweat every night, needing to purge my skin of the horrible feeling of death cooling her fingers in mine.

Had Adelaide been an acquaintance of Dr. Harrison's before I'd passed my powers to him? I had yet to meet a person who liked him for anything but his money, and I didn't see my girl taking his wealth and pretentiousness into consideration.

Still, I imagined I was the last person she wanted to see. I'd promised to protect her, to be her husband for better and worse. Instead, I'd been unable to heal her, left her in our bedchamber without a goodbye, and forced her into a marriage she couldn't possibly want. I didn't expect her to forgive me for that.

I'd done the only thing I could do, and my sacrifice hadn't been in vain. My sisters would live well a while longer, even if Livvie was back in service at the Library.

And Adelaide was healing.

Still, I longed to see proof that she lived. If I could feel the warmth of her skin, would it erase the horror of death in my memories?

I surveyed my surroundings and saw no guards, but that didn't mean there were none. Under cover of darkness, I moved to the back of the house. I slipped through the gardens towards the spot where I'd first climbed the wall to meet Adelaide.

Could I still get inside the Fairshaw Library, or did her feelings no longer sway the Fairshaw magic? There was just one way to find out.

Chapter 36

Frederick

Knelt on the hardwood floor by the side of Adelaide's bed, I watched as she slept. Her chest rose and fell steadily. Pale lashes rested against cheeks that were rosier than I'd seen them for a long time. Her hair was no longer matted, but shone in the flickering light from the candle I'd lit.

She looked like the woman I'd first laid eyes on—young, healthy. *And full of life.*

So different from the dying one I'd left to save.

The tight knot in my chest eased, and my breath came easily for the first time since I'd left. I'd hoped she'd send for me once she'd regained her strength. But I also knew the only thing allowing me to sneak undetected into the Fairshaw Library like I had, would be a Fairshaw wanting me here. And that Fairshaw was not Dr. Harrison. *Somewhere in her heart there must be love for me still.*

I took comfort in that thought as I reached out a hand

to caress a silky lock of her hair. She let out a low moan. A frown spread across her forehead, and her nose crinkled. *Could she feel my presence?* I released her hair.

I had no claim to her anymore, but my body didn't seem to know that. The mere thought of Dr. Harrison's hands all over my bride was enough to make my blood boil. Enough to make me want to carry her out of here in my arms, spend whatever time I needed to convince her to run away with me. Surely we could make our way out of Fairshaw undetected. *We could go to London, get lost in the crowds, make a new life where no one knew us.*

Adelaide's lashes fluttered, and I froze. Should I run before she had the guards called? Or, worse, her husband? Whether he slept in her room or not, I doubted he'd be pleased to find me here.

She blinked and opened her eyes. But her gaze held no fear, nor the anger I'd expected. My name on her lips was a benediction. "Frederick?"

All thoughts of guards forgotten, I bent closer. "Yes, love."

Her eyes widened, and a spark of hope lit in their blue depths. "You love me?"

Had she thought I didn't? Why else would I have given up everything I'd worked for? I longed to touch her, but would she welcome it? I rose on my knees and leaned closer. "Of course I do."

She frowned. "I asked for you every day. I thought if you didn't even bother to see if I was better…" Her words halted.

That filthy Dr. Harrison! "Nobody told me, love."

Her face softened, and she shifted. Her cool fingers against my temple—*sweet mercy!*—were like the touch of an angel. "You're really here. I thought maybe you were a dream."

I groaned and rested my forehead against hers. "I'm so sorry I didn't come sooner. If I'd had any idea you'd asked for me…" I clamped my mouth shut on the string of curses I'd like to call down on her husband. She didn't deserve my ire—and it wasn't meant for her.

I pulled back. Her clear blue eyes were no longer glassy like when she'd tried to say goodbye to me. "I don't understand why I am married to Dr. Harrison and not you. Did you not want me?" *Oh, if only.*

I reached out to touch her cheek. Her eyelids fluttered, then closed as my fingers ran over the soft skin of her jaw, her neck. *Touching her was heaven.* "I *only* wanted you. I thought if I sacrificed what I wanted most, it would break the link between you and the Fairshaw Cat. And if I was wrong, I needed him to have a compelling reason to heal you." I credited the Fairshaw magic for the idea I'd never have come up with myself.

She frowned, and all I wanted was to kiss that frown off her beautiful face—kiss her until she forgot how to frown at all. "What if you'd been wrong?"

Pain jammed into my chest. "It wouldn't have made much of a difference at the time."

She let out a derisive snort. "Except that I would have died married to Dr. Harrison."

I fought a smile at her indignation, but it disappeared as I remembered how close she'd come to losing her life. "The important word here being 'died', not 'married'."

Adelaide rolled her eyes, and a grin stretched my cheeks. *God, I'd missed her feistiness.* I slipped a hand along her jaw, framing her face. She pressed her cheek into my palm, and the feel of her silky skin against mine was almost too much to handle. "How is he treating you?"

I wasn't sure I was ready to hear her answer. If he was mistreating her in any way, so help me God—

"He treats me well." Her words put my fears to rest. "He gives me sleeping draughts, so I don't see him much." Unease rose in my chest. *Why did he need her asleep? It had been weeks. Surely she'd recovered enough to not need the forced rest?* She hesitated, and I felt my blood pressure rise again.

234

"What?"

"He…refuses to tell me where you are. And he's being secretive about how the dissolution of our marriage is to happen."

Cold settled in my stomach. "Dissolution?" I croaked the words.

"He says he'll divorce me, rather than get an annulment." She frowned. "But he's given me no other details." I felt the blood leave my face, and the curse that fell from my lips was weak. *Had the doctor's brews addled her mind? How had she not recognized his lies immediately?* I opened my mouth, but the words refused to come.

How could I trash the hope on her face and squash the life I finally saw in her again? But I couldn't lie to her—not after what my last omission had put us through. I rose from the floor and seated myself on the edge of her bed. Was Dr. Harrison really planning to kill her? But men had done worse for power.

"Frederick?" Her voice filled with the same fear that shadowed her eyes. "What are you not telling me?"

"There's no dissolution, Adelaide. Fairshaw marriages can't be dissolved—other than by death." Her face blanched. "He's trying to *kill* me?"

I nodded. Her curse was low and tears sprang to her eyes as she reached for me. I folded her into my arms, and her face pressed against my neck as her tears wet my shirt collar, burning me. How could I have been so careless with her? I'd tried to save her, and instead I'd put her in more danger.

"I won't let him hurt you, love." I had no idea how I'd keep a promise like that, but I swore I would find a way. I crawled into her bed and slipped under the covers, kissed the tears away from her cheeks, and whispered soft words into her hair. Tightening my grip around her, I held her until she fell asleep.

But I couldn't sleep. *How could I when her life was in danger?*

CHAPTER 37

Frederick

The most powerful man in Fairshaw was planning to kill my bride. Sure, by law she may be his wife, but she was the woman I loved. I had sacrificed everything for her, only to push her into the hands of a murderer.

Worried my lack of sleep would cause a misstep on the treacherous vine, I made my way down the hall towards the front of the Library. I stepped out through the mahogany doors of the Fairshaw Library as the first rays of sunlight hit the carved stone steps. No guards flanked the doors, and the only servant I'd seen was the Fairshaws' butler. *Had he'd heard my steps and kept his back to me on purpose? Did that mean Adelaide still had allies in her home?*

If the Fairshaw had known who'd held his wife as she drifted off to sleep last night, he'd be less lackadaisical about his guards. Did he not know the magic followed not only his wishes, but Adelaide's too? How was he the Fairshaw Master without that knowledge?

The clocktower struck the time, but the number of chimes had no meaning. What was time when I had no way to thwart my wife's would-be murderer?

Leaving Adelaide behind killed me, but I didn't know how to bring her with me safely. Not alone. Not when this man had any number of guards and staff at his disposal. That they weren't posted at the entrance didn't mean they couldn't be called on a moment's notice.

Another thought crashed into my tired brain, and fear chilled my blood. *My sister was still at the Library.* If Dr. Harrison was willing to kill his wife, what kind of damage would he inflict on an orphan girl from the docks? Liv would have to come home. I'd send Martha for her after breakfast. Hopefully she'd get a better reception from the butler than I had.

Moving one foot in front of the other as if in a daze, I made my way along the cobbled streets through town, until I found myself at the front stoop of my sister's shabby apartment. I'd stayed away since I'd moved out of the Library. There were plenty of places better suited to sleep off a raging hangover.

Without knocking, I entered the dimly lit room to the sound of a scuffle and a shutting door. I frowned and lifted my gaze in time to see a disheveled Martha jump out from around the corner that led to the bedroom. She stumbled towards me, a blush darkening her cheeks. "Frederick! I didn't...expect you. You haven't been here for so long!"

I shrugged, tossed my cap at the nail on the wall and missed. It dropped onto the hard stamped dirt floor, and I sank into one of the three chairs at the table. My forehead dropped into my hands.

"What's wrong?" Martha's voice softened as she stepped closer. Her hand dropped to my shoulder, moving in comforting circles across my shoulders and back like it had so many times over the years. But her comfort wasn't enough this time.

"Dr. Harrison is trying to kill his wife." Her movement ceased, and I caught her frown as I glanced over my shoulder. "*My* wife. Adelaide."

Her eyes lit with understanding, then anger. "That filthy bastard!"

I'd never heard Martha curse in all the years I'd lived under her roof, but here she was, sounding so much like Adelaide my heart hurt.

"What do I do, Martha?" I wanted advice from the girl who'd had no shortage of it when I'd gotten into scrapes as a child. But this was so much more than a scrape. I'd told Adelaide I would figure this out, but I had no clue how I'd go about it. I'd found a solution to her dying easily when I'd had the Fairshaw magic's knowledge and power on my side, but this time? "He's trying to kill her, and he's the Fairshaw with complete access and control over her. How do I keep her safe?"

Martha's hand took up its soothing motion again. "Adelaide is a Fairshaw by blood, so wouldn't she have kept her magic?"

I shook my head. "He keeps her incapacitated with some kind of strong medicine. It must be addling her brain because I had to tell her Fairshaw marriages couldn't be dissolved by divorce like he'd told her." Martha started to speak, but a crash from the backroom interrupted her. I pushed my chair away and stood, almost knocking my sister over. "Is anyone else here?"

This was supposed to be a private conversation, but Martha lived alone, so I hadn't expected there to be anyone else here. Not this early. I glanced from the back of the apartment to Martha's pinking cheeks.

"I'm here. I should have made myself known." The blacksmith's son emerged from her bedroom, a sheepish smile on his face. He and I had played together as children, but the broad shoulders in front of me didn't belong to a child. And the way he looked at my sister didn't either.

"Nicholas? Why would you be here alone with my sister?" *Right—there were a million reasons why a man would be alone with a woman in the predawn hours.* I, myself, had left my wife behind in our bed minutes ago.

Except, as far as I knew, Nicholas Cromwell had no such claim on my sister. I remembered the shuffling noises I'd heard when I'd entered and Martha's disheveled appearance, and turned a sharp glare on the man I'd grown up with. "Listen—"

"Frederick." My sister's voice held exasperation, and a warning.

I barreled on, ignoring the way her boot tapped the dirt floor. "How long has this been going on?"

Nicholas opened his mouth, but Martha was faster. "He's helped with…little things here and there since Liv moved into the Library, and—"

"What? That's been months! Were you going to tell me?"

Martha's expression shifted from flustered to stern, and her voice was the one she'd used that time when I'd torn my last shirt straight down the back in a street brawl. "Frederick James Holloway, you do not own me. I do not need to inform you of every little change around here. Especially when you've got your own household."

I scowled at Nicholas, but there was no heat in it. He didn't return my anger, but squared his shoulders. "I would have told you, Mr. Holloway."

Martha glared at him. "You can call him Frederick."

I rolled my eyes. I didn't have time for this. "Martha, need you to go to the Library and bring Liv home."

Nicholas stepped forward, brow furrowed. "Is she all right?" The concern in his voice made me like him more. Though I still resented his going behind my back.

"I don't know. But I don't want her in the household of a madman."

Martha dipped her head to glance out the window, already reaching for the knit shawl tossed over a chair across from me. She wrapped it around herself. "I should be able to go soon." Suddenly my strong sister looked so vulnerable. Her slender fingers trembled as she knotted the fabric around her thin waist. I moved to wrap an arm around her, but found I was no longer needed.

Nicholas' large hand already rested on her shoulder, his thumb drawing circles over the worn shawl. "She'll be all right. We'll get her." His words were whispered, but it was impossible not to overhear them. Martha's shoulders sank under his touch, and the lines between her brows eased.

What had she said? That I had my own household to worry about now? Sure, I did. Until Dr. Harrison succeeded in killing my wife. I groaned, louder than I'd meant to, I realized, when both Martha and Nicholas turned.

Martha's eyes softened. "How are you going to stop him?"

I shook my head. "I don't know how!" I shoved my hand through my hair again, but the action brought no relief. "She's *my wife*. I'm supposed to be protecting her, and here this bastard is, poisoning her before my very eyes. I need to get her out of there."

I looked to Nicholas. Would he have my back? He dipped his head, but there were still just the two of us. Who knew how many guards the Fairshaw Library employed?

"Wait until Liv is safe, Frederick." Alarm filled Martha's voice.

I nodded. "You go first, and once Liv is back here, I'm getting my wife."

And then there was the small matter that she wasn't actually my wife anymore, but his. Could I find a way to change that? Again?

CHAPTER 38

Adelaide

I woke up with a dull ache in my head. Disoriented, my eyes flitted over shining mahogany furniture, the tidy stack of books on the desk, the heavy drapes covering the windows of my bedchamber. No, not mine. Ours. I'd slept here for weeks, and it had only felt like home on the morning when I'd woken up wrapped in Frederick's arms. Since then? Not so much.

I frowned, and the movement felt like an anvil to my forehead. I immediately relaxed my facial muscles. I'd slept better than I had in weeks, and the splitting headache made no sense. I'd fretted about Frederick's whereabouts before going to sleep. And then...then I'd dreamed of him. No. Not a dream. Twisting to the side, I ran my fingers over the faint imprint of a head on the pillow next to me.

Frederick *had* been here.

I rolled over, smashed my face into the soft fabric and

was rewarded with the smell of him. *I hadn't dreamed it. I'd fallen asleep in his wonderful, strong arms.* The beat of the heart that held mine completely in real life had followed me into my dreams. I'd missed him so much, and now I had to miss him still. The pillow dampened under my cheek.

He'd told me something important, but what? We'd talked before he'd crawled into my bed, hadn't we? I shook my head to dislodge the fog. The pain was immediate, and I whimpered. Then, the fog cleared and our conversation entered my mind with shattering clarity.

"Fairshaw marriages can't be dissolved—other than by death."

My pulse hammered in my throat. *Oh, God. Dr. Harrison was planning to kill me. I couldn't let him kill me.* Breathing slowly in through my nose, I tried to calm my frantic nerves.

Frederick wouldn't let him hurt me. But what could *he* really do? He was no longer the Fairshaw Master, and the power-hungry man with the title held all the cards. Dr. Harrison was everything I'd once accused Frederick of. I'd been so terribly wrong about the man that had sacrificed all his power and wealth to save me. I groaned—then moaned from the pain the sound caused.

The door opened, admitting the last person I wanted

to see. "How did you sleep, love?" Dr. Harrison's voice was the kind one would expect from a newly-wed husband. Except that he held no such tender feelings for me. Why did he suddenly feel the need to use endearments?

The reason appeared directly behind him, flushed and holding a jug of steaming water. Elizabeth. "M'lady, I tried to tell Master Fairshaw you would prefer the chance to wash up before his audience, but he seems unable to fathom it."

Dr. Harrison's jaw clenched. What must have passed between them for her to dare say something like that to him? I had never heard Elizabeth be impertinent before, and as her master, he could have her punished severely. Would he? Hoping to save Elizabeth, I turned to Dr. Harrison with a smile, and the pain in my head was blinding. "You wanted to speak to me, husband?" I forced the words out, even as the title scorched my throat.

"I did want to speak to you. Although if you would rather wait until after your maid's ministrations, I don't mind waiting."

Was he not going to give me the privacy to wash up? But he made no move to leave. I swallowed. "I would like to hear you out, please."

Elizabeth's face fell, but she spoke up. "The water will cool, M'lady."

What was wrong with her? I didn't dare meet her eyes under Dr. Harrison's scrutiny, but she needed to stop before he had her sacked.

"Elizabeth." I cleared my throat, willing my voice to sound sincere. "You may leave the water here, and I will make do." Dr. Harrison looked marginally pleased at this, but Elizabeth's eyes were pure fire. I had never seen her like this.

"M'lady." She curtsied, and walked into the room to place her jug on the bedside table. Livvie followed her with an armful of fresh towels and a petrified expression on her face. Elizabeth deposited the jug, and her eyes searched the area around my bed. "This chamber pot needs emptying."

Livvie started forward, but Elizabeth shoved her back. "I've got it." She all but sneered at the young girl, and Livvie's eyes filled with tears.

My mouth dropped open. *Was my maid possessed?* I couldn't believe what I was seeing. I'd never heard her raise her voice to Livvie. I shot the little girl an apologetic look as Elizabeth bent close by my bed to grab the pan underneath it.

"What is wrong with you?" I didn't care that I sounded angry.

"Don't trust him. He wants to—"

"I believe the bedpan can wait." Dr. Harrison's cold voice cut her off, and suddenly he stood next to us. Elizabeth's face went so white I thought she would faint. I grabbed for her arm, but Dr. Harrison was faster, gripping her other arm so tightly she winced. "You have other pressing duties, maid." His venomous words held a clear threat, and it pulled the last of the fire from my maid. Suddenly, she seemed vulnerable.

I wanted to pull her into my arms like she'd done for me so many times, but fear held me back. What would Dr. Harrison do to her if I angered him?

"Yes, Master Fairshaw." Elizabeth's words were slurred. Leaning on a deathly pale Livvie, she staggered to the door.

Fear slithered down my back. "What is wrong with her?" Dr. Harrison shrugged, but a blue glow surrounded him, and I understood why Elizabeth's flare of temper had disappeared. *He'd shocked her with magic.*

The hatred I had felt toward him before had nothing on the emotions that charged through me at this moment. *Burning, withering, blazing.*

I closed my eyes, terrified of what he might see in them. *He hurt my maid,* my friend, *with magic.*

Edward Fairshaw might have been an unfair master at times—difficult to please and eager to find fault. I'd felt the brunt of both his displeasure and ignorance. But he had never, *never*, used his magic to hurt me or his staff. Hatred like I'd never felt before chilled my blood.

Ice pushed through my veins.

Fire ignited in my hands.

Magic surged inside me.

I wanted to hurt him. This man did not deserve to be the Fairshaw Master. He didn't even deserve to move his filthy feet across the Library floors.

"Lady Fairshaw?" Back was his usual address for me, and it took all my strength not to sneer at him. I needed to tamp down my magic—I couldn't show a man who wanted me dead that I had any powers at all.

As if invisible hands closed over the source, the ice in my veins disappeared and the fire under my skin cooled, leaving only a faint buzz behind. I opened my eyes, and found Dr. Harrison's narrowed on me.

"I'm not feeling well." I winced at the words, like I would have when I woke up.

His shoulders sank in obvious relief. Had he seen my burst of magic? "I will make you more of my brew."

I didn't bother with a smile this time. Let him think I was too sick to plaster one on. "Thank you." I sank against the pillows again. I really did feel unwell—as if my uncanny burst of magic had sapped all the energy sleep had restored. "What did you want to talk about?"

His face turned blank. "It's no matter, just the terms of our divorce, but we will wait until you feel better." *Did he mean until I was dead?*

I grimaced. "I have a terrible headache. Can you send me my lady's maid later?"

His eyes lit with anger for a moment before the emotionless mask returned. "I don't think she's fit to be your maid anymore."

Oh no. He wouldn't sack her, would he? Real tears sprang into my eyes. "Please. I've known her since we were both children. Even if not as a servant, it would comfort me to have her here with me."

He seemed to think it over, and then he nodded. "Well, then. I will send her to see you."

CHAPTER 39

Adelaide

lizabeth stepped into my room, a shell of the woman I'd known all my life. In vain I tried to catch her eyes, tried to make or answer my questions about her earlier outburst. What had she tried to say before Dr. Harrison had silenced her?

My head still pounded. I pressed my thumb and fingers to my temples and let out a deep breath. "Strip out of your clothes, please, Elizabeth."

She gasped, eyes wide. "What?"

"I want to see that there are no bruises on your body."

Tears sprang to Elizabeth's eyes, and I almost took back my words. She shook her head. "He is the Fairshaw Master, and you think he would need to use his fists to harm me?"

But I'd seen the anger in his eyes, felt the evil coming off of him in waves as his knuckles had paled around her arm. "Please, Elizabeth. I need to know."

She unbuttoned her bodice and let it fall to the floor. Her skirt followed. She raised the sleeves and hem of her shift until I was satisfied she bore no marks.

Now my eyes were the ones brimming with tears. *If her bruises were not outward, they must be much worse.* "What did he *do* to you?"

She only shook her head, and I looked around for Livvie. She would tell me if she knew, but she wasn't in the room. "Where's Livvie? Is she with him?"

Pain darkened Elizabeth's eyes, and my chest shriveled. She made no move to answer, but the tears that leaked from her eyes told me everything I needed to know.

I was going to kill him.

How dare he use a child to manipulate Elizabeth? And what had he threatened to do to her? Fear chilled my blood. I needed to get Livvie away from the Library. Once she was safe, I'd deal with the miserable excuse of a human that had stolen my husband's title. He'd never intended to honor his side of the bargain with Frederick—he didn't deserve to be the Fairshaw Master.

But would the Fairshaw magic help me defeat him, or come to his aid?

CHAPTER 40

Adelaide

My door pushed open again, and Dr. Harrison entered. I couldn't think of him as my husband—the thought was so vile. I loved Frederick regardless of his last name, and while I didn't blame him for the sacrifice that had saved my life, I was irked to be stuck with such a slimy creature of a man. And worse than slimy—one willing to threaten harm to a child.

"Where is my youngest maid?"

"Who?" He might pretend he couldn't keep our servants apart, but I didn't miss the calculating gleam in his eyes.

"My older maid seems a bit…ill of ease, and I thought perhaps I could replace the younger one in her position." The lie hurt. I could never replace Elizabeth—as my friend or maid, but I needed to make sure Livvie was safe.

"What should become of your older maid?"

"No harm!" I felt the sparks along my neck as I barely kept the panic from my voice. "Please don't harm her. She may no longer be fit to serve as a lady's maid, but I don't want anything to happen to her."

He dipped his head. "Very well." But I didn't trust him for a second. Sparks skittered across my skin. I needed to get rid of this man who seemed to activate my magic in a way I'd never felt before.

"I feel quite sick. Perhaps you could send my younger maid to aid me?" He nodded, a satisfied expression on his face. Because the teas he brewed me were working like they were supposed to? I shuddered as a chill snaked over my skin. *This man who was supposed to heal me, supposed to protect me*, smiled *at the thought of my death.*

The door closed behind him, and I breathed a sigh of relief. Now I only needed Livvie. He wouldn't have harmed her, would he? Not as long as Elizabeth had gone along with his wishes? My hands trembled, drawing my attention to the blue light dancing along my fingertips. *What was this?*

I'd been born a Fairshaw, and I'd always felt the Fairshaw magic in my blood. But it had been a slow tingle, not the sensations I now felt. Why did I suddenly display visible signs of magic? My thoughts spun as I tried to make sense of it all. A soft knock on the door interrupted me.

"Enter."

The door moved and Livvie pushed through the small space between the door and jamb. "M'lady, Master Fairshaw said you wanted to see me?"

I sank against the headboard, and relief brought tears to my eyes. "Livvie! You're unharmed!" I sat up as she closed the door and crossed the floor. I didn't like her furtive glances over her shoulder. Was she worried someone would barge in on us?

When she reached the side of my bed, her dark eyes were wary. "M'lady, what happened to Miss Elizabeth? She's crying in the kitchen." Her voice trembled, and anger surged in me. How dare he scare her?

Livvie's eyes moved up from mine and widened. "M'lady, your hair!"

More magic? I reached up to touch my hair, but felt the sparks in the air long before my fingertips made contact. I knew for certain my magic had never been visible to others, and my mind spun with the only possibility I could think of. "Don't worry, Livvie. I'm sure it will go away soon." *And hopefully before Dr. Harrison realized that I had more magic than he did. Did I?*

I motioned Livvie closer. "I need you to carry a message to your sister, Martha. I'd like to thank her for her hospitality before my wedding." I took care not to use the

Holloway name. It wouldn't surprise me if Dr. Harrison had ears posted outside my door.

I opened my arms to Livvie and, after a moment's hesitation, she came right into them. Hugging her little body close, I whispered into her ear. "When you get to Martha, stay with her. Don't return to the Library unless Frederick or I come and get you."

She pulled away a little, but kept her voice low. "You still love Frederick, then?" The hope in her eyes made mine sting. Had she really thought I'd forgotten all about her brother?

"Always." The love that bloomed in my heart echoed in my voice. I turned her toward the door. "Now, hurry."

She ran across the floor and closed the door behind her. I sank back against the headboard and prayed she would make it unhindered to Pendle Street and that Martha would keep her from returning to the Library.

My eyelids fluttered with exhaustion—just this short interaction with Livvie seemed to have drained my energy. Dr. Harrison's teas might not have killed me as they were surely meant to, but I felt now how they must have chipped away at my health. I could think more clearly for each hour that passed without exposure to his medicine. Gone was the fog that hid the last few weeks from my memories, and finally I began to understand.

I pressed my hands to my white coverlet, fascinated with the blue tint visible under my fingernails. Was my suspicion right? It must be—the events of the last few weeks only made sense in the light of it.

I cursed the man who'd drugged me for so long. If he hadn't, would I have figured it out sooner? That I didn't need to stay shackled to him, or any man?

The freedom I'd longed for since my father's death was finally in reach. Power surged under my skin as the Fairshaw magic flowed through my veins—and there was no doubt in my mind what had happened.

CHAPTER 41

Frederick

An object crashed against the outside of the door to my sister's home, and the planks shook from the impact. Startled, I stood from my seat at the table. Nicholas and Martha did the same as the door opened, and Liv came barging through the opening, heaving for breath.

I was next to her in a second. "Liv! What's wrong? Is something the matter with Adelaide?" She doubled over, gasping for air and shaking her head. I knelt by her side. "Why aren't you at the Library?" *Surely the housekeeper hadn't absolved her of her duties?*

"Mistress…sent me here—" Another gasp. "Stay till you or she—"

Martha wrapped her arm around Liv's thin shoulders. "Let her catch her breath, Frederick."

My jaw ached as I tried to keep from saying words I knew I'd regret. The very thought of Dr. Harrison wanting to kill my wife made anger surge through my body. Anger neither of my sisters deserved.

"Mistress Adelaide sent me here and said not to return unless she or—" Liv blew out a breath. "Unless she or you came to fetch me."

I frowned. "Why would she need you to stay away from the Library? Are you not safe there?"

Liv's eyes filled with tears, and Martha's face blanched. "Liv. What are you not telling us?"

Her face crumpled, and tears gathered on her lashes, streaking down through the dirt on her cheeks. "I think Master Harrison, I mean Fairshaw, did something bad to Elizabeth."

My stomach sank. "Adelaide's lady's maid? Why would he hurt *her*?" Elizabeth was fiercely loyal to Adelaide, if Dr. Harrison was going after her maid, it didn't bode well for my wife.

She sniffled. "He didn't want her to talk to M'lady, but she did anyway. And Master did something to her."

"Did what?" Martha and I spoke at the same time.

Liv shrugged and wiped her sleeve under her nose. "He held her arm and made her shiver, and it hurt her terribly."

Ice filled my stomach. *Magic.* And the man who'd recklessly used it against Adelaide's maid was the most powerful man in the town of Fairshaw.

Martha's brows pulled into a worried frown. Nicholas stepped close and wrapped his arm around her shoulders. He was no longer the quiet blacksmith's son who'd run barefoot by my side through the Fairshaw woods when we were children. But he'd had my back then, and I didn't think that had changed. "I'm getting Adelaide out of there now Liv's safe."

Nicholas nodded. "I'll go with you." Martha let out a sound of protest, but Nicholas pressed his fingers against her cheek in a caress I knew I ought to look away from. "I'll make it back to you, love."

My oldest sister pulled in a deep breath and turned to press her lips to his fingers. She held his gaze for a long moment as magic sparked in the air around them.

No, not magic.

Love.

He bent his head towards her, and I finally averted my eyes. When I turned back, Martha was seated and pulling Liv into her lap.

When all this was over, I had so many questions for my sister, but first, I had a wife to rescue.

I turned to Nicholas. "Tonight. We'll have to go in after dark."

He gave a short nod. "How will we get in?" I filled him in on where I'd found Adelaide last night, and how we'd enter the Library unseen. It wasn't much of a plan. But if I could keep from losing my mind while I waited for nightfall, it might just work.

CHAPTER 42

Adelaide

D
r. Harrison returned with his cursed brew twice more before nightfall, and both times I managed to soak the contents into the mattress without his noticing. When he inquired about my health, I told him I felt worse. I wanted to smack the somber expression off his face, but I couldn't let on what I knew, or what kind of power I held—not yet.

No doubt Dr. Harrison had magic of his own, if not Fairshaw magic, and I couldn't confront him until I was stronger.

Darkness crept through the window panes in my bedchamber, tinting the sheer inner curtains a soft blue. Quiet footsteps alerted me to his presence much too late, and it took all my strength to keep from calling out my surprise. "One last brew for the night, Lady Fairshaw. I'm thinking tomorrow you'll be feeling much better."

Did he mean *dead*? Nausea rose in my throat, but I feigned a yawn. "I feel so sleepy."

It was too dark to see his show of concern. "Yes, that's good... To be expected for certain, but you'll need to drink this." He handed me a cup of truly foul smelling liquid.

I let my hand tremble as I took the cup from him. "I will. I feel awful." Certain he bought my fake gulps, I pulled the coverlet close to my cup and tilted the mug against it. Some of it dripped down, wetting my nightgown, and my disgusted expression was real. "Ugh, it tastes terrible."

He nodded, pleased. "I determined you needed something stronger. You haven't...improved...as fast as I hoped." One last false swallow, and I returned the cup to him, my hands shaking—but this time with anger. He stepped back. "Goodnight, wife."

I shuddered, and mumbled an answer. Satisfied, he turned and left the room as quietly as he'd come.

Hiding my powers required considerable effort, and as the door closed behind Dr. Harrison, exhaustion wrapped around me like a heavy blanket. As soon as my full strength returned, I would go find the man I'd marry regardless of title—his *or* mine. But just now my eyelids were too heavy. I'd rest them a bit first.

A hand rested against my forehead. Was Dr. Harrison checking to see if I was cold yet? What would he do if I wasn't? What would *I* do if he tried to overpower me? "Adelaide."

No. That voice belonged to another man—the one I loved. I opened my eyes, but was only rewarded with darkness. "Frederick?"

"It's me." His voice wasn't the free, carefree one I'd come to love. I felt his unease in his every movement, more so as he reached for me. "Why is your bed wet—" He cursed. "Adelaide!"

"Shh. It's Dr. Harrison's tea. I couldn't drink it, so I needed to pour it somewhere."

I felt his breath of relief against my forehead as he pulled me from the bed and into his arms. "Thank God. I thought it was blood, or... I thought you were about to—" His mouth closed on his next words, and he pressed a kiss to my temple.

"I'm well, Frederick." He nodded and clutched me harder against his chest.

"Everything all right?" A low voice sounded from the window, and I nearly screamed. A guard?

"Yes, everything is well. Come on!" Why had Frederick brought another man to see me?

I heard movement, and then a grunt of frustration. "I can't get in. There is some sort of barrier."

"Adelaide. He's a friend, can you let him in?"

"Of course." *But how did I use this power?* I was about to ask Frederick, but in the next moment, the man's boots hit the floor, and he closed the distance between us.

I nudged Frederick. "Are you going to put me down so I can walk?"

I felt more than saw him shake his head. "In case we get caught it needs to look like we're taking you against your will. I don't want to give him a reason to retaliate against you."

I scoffed. "Retaliate *more* than trying to kill me?"

Frederick stiffened. "Shh. Don't think about that. We'll get you out of here." The other man moved toward the door to the hallway.

"Frederick, wait. Use the servants' passage." I gestured toward the wallpapered door by the fireplace.

"It's too small. We won't be able to move fast enough." Frederick's breath warmed my ear. I took in the hulking form of his friend and knew he was right. We couldn't waste time. How long did we have until Dr. Harrison discovered I was gone? Until his guards realized there were intruders in the Library?

Frederick's friend peeked out the door, and on his signal, we moved into the hallway. What time was it? From the heaviness in my body, I guessed past midnight. Did the Fairshaw guards still follow the schedule they'd had while my father was alive, or had Dr. Harrison changed that too? If their duties had remained unchanged, there would only be guards outside the room where the Fairshaw slept. I dearly hoped it was still so.

Whatever the case, there were no guards stationed in this hallway at the moment. We moved with stealth along the endless corridor. Frederick's heart pounded against the side of my ribs, his arms wrapped around me as if they had the ability to protect me from harm. *If only they did.*

We entered another long hall, but no servants appeared, neither did we see any guards. A door creaked, and Frederick turned us towards the sound.

"Fools. She'll be dead before daybreak." Dr. Harrison's voice was foreboding and emotionless, like a chill in the air. His laugh, devoid of happiness, filled the hall. "I've killed her just like I killed the damned Fairshaw Cat." I gasped, and Frederick's body tensed against me. He turned, and I saw the man who could never be my husband emerge from a doorway down the hall.

The name Frederick called him made Dr. Harrison's pale face redden. "I begged you to save her and you tried to kill her!"

"And I succeeded—you'll see come morning." The pitiful imposter took another step forward.

I wriggled in Frederick's arms. "Put me down, so I can deal with him."

"I don't want you to have to deal with him ever again." His arms tightened around me and remorse joined the fury in his voice. "I gave him the key. The Fairshaw Cat died protecting it, and I handed it to him like the fool I am."

I slid a hand up his neck, and felt the trembling of his skin. "Frederick, you didn't know. And you did save my life like you set out to do. Now, let me handle him." A tremble ran through my body as all around us the wall sconces lit with wildly flickering flames. The same hue that glowed faintly where my hand touched my husband's skin. *My true husband, the one I'd vowed to love.*

The blue light flickered across Dr. Harrison's frown as he stepped back. "What is this?"

"Are you doing this, love?" Frederick's voice was an awed whisper.

"Yes. Now, let me down." My feet hit the floor, but Frederick's hands were still on me. I swayed, and they settled on my hips. "Don't let go." I needed his support.

Magic surged through my blood, but I wasn't sure I had the strength to stand upright on my own.

"I won't let go, wife." His voice was thick. *Wife.* The word thrummed through my body, igniting my blood. Swirls of magic gathered in my chest, mixing with rising anger.

This was what Dr. Harrison had taken away from me. The presence of this man who stood behind me after the accusations I'd thrown at him, his steady hands holding me up when I couldn't stand. This love.

The light in the wall sconces flickered out, plunging the hallway into complete darkness.

"What is the meaning of this? Guards!" Dr. Harrison's last word was a bellow, but I heard the fear in his voice. *Fear of me.*

Magic sparkled along the surface of my skin, flickering, burning, freezing. Frederick let out a gasp behind me, but his hands stayed clamped on my hips.

"Guards!" I relished the weakness in Dr. Harrison's voice. The lights flickered once, then went out again.

"What's the matter, *husband, d*oes your magic not work against mine? Do you not have the Fairshaw magic you murdered to own?"

I felt the power I'd sensed in my father deep inside my bones. I was stronger than ever—strong enough to pull on the full magic of the Fairshaw Library—mine by marriage and sacrifice.

The glow from my skin lit the hallway. Dr. Harrison's face was a grimace of pain, and his screams echoed through the air. He slumped to his knees and writhed on the ground. *He deserved to writhe. He'd killed the magical cat. He'd tried to kill me, terrified Elizabeth, threatened to hurt Livvie. I hated him.*

Hated *him.*

His howls of agony rose, and fire replaced my blood. *This vengeance was mine.*

"Adelaide!" Frederick's shout sounded far away, as if his voice was a slow fog, seeping between the trees of a forest to reach me. He repeated my name, and an object crashed to the ground in front of me, shattering the floor. An increasingly loud rumble filled the room. "You need to stop! You're killing us!"

What?

I forced the power away from Dr. Harrison's body to light the wall sconces, and gasped at the scene in front of me. The hall was transformed. Piles of dust and debris covered once pristine carpets. The wall on my left side was broken and the room beyond it, as ruined as the hall. I looked at my arms and found them coated with a fine dust, then glanced to Dr. Harrison. Slumped on the floor in the doorway he'd entered to gloat, he didn't move.

Quiet thundered in my ears. I no longer felt Frederick's hands on my hips and spun around. *Where was he?* Why couldn't I hear him calling my name anymore?

Dust swirled in the air, clogging my throat and making my eyes water. I covered my mouth with a gritty hand.

"Adelaide." I ran towards Frederick's groan. A shadow emerged from the fog, and as I closed in, I recognized Frederick's torn, bloodied hand. His tendons strained as he pressed against a section of wall pinning the man who'd accompanied us.

I gasped. "What do I do?"

"Trying not to kill this man would be a good start." His breath was labored, but no sound came from the man underneath the debris. *Was it already too late?*

And how was I supposed to help? "I don't know how to use the magic!"

"You need to figure it out." He grunted the words through gritted teeth. "You'll cause my sister a life of heartache if you don't."

I closed my eyes, searching for the wisdom that accompanied the magic. Hatred for Dr. Harrison had guided it to destruction. Could an equally strong emotion guide it towards healing?

Compassion? Was this man Miss Holloway's secret beau that had listened to our conversation through her back-door? I pictured her dark eyes filled with tears and tried to imagine her grief if this man didn't make it. Frederick let out another groan, desperation coloring his voice. "It's not working, Adelaide. Try something else. You're killing me."

But I couldn't focus on his words. Not when the pink light of morning burst through the broken stained glass windows above us, tinting the destruction all around me. The words of another man echoed through my mind. *"She'll be dead before daybreak."*

Grief knocked me to my knees.

I'd come too close to losing Frederick tonight. If I had drunk the last of Dr. Harrison's brews, would I already be dead? Pain stretched around me, sharp, tight, and deadly. It tore into my chest as I collapsed on the ground.

The floor rumbled again as magic forced its way through my tendons, under my skin, into every strand of my hair. I cried out from the intensity. Muffled curses sounded close by. Then a groan, and a weight hit the floor. The impact reverberated into the ground, my knees, my bones. My hollow mind.

"She'll be dead."

The power that coursed through me refused to separate

from the grief I'd called forth. The Library hall faded around me, and I saw Frederick's stricken face as the Fairshaw magic locked the window between us—forever separating us. My heart cracked open like it had when he'd entered the chapel an hour later and I knew for sure he'd murdered for greed. Was this what dying felt like?

I sobbed his name over and over. "I can't... I can't lose you again."

Muffled words faded into footsteps, and then strong arms wrapped around my torso. "You won't lose me. I'm here." Frederick's large hand cradled the back of my head. "I've got you."

I cried in his arms as his soothing whispers warmed my ear. His hand stroked my hair, and my sobs stilled. I pulled in air still tainted with dust and coughed. But as my cough eased, I pulled in another breath, and another. *Life* thrummed through my veins, danced over my skin.

I wasn't dying.

Had Frederick left his friend behind to get to me? Or had my grief moved the Fairshaw magic to heal? I opened my eyes, but my lashes only brushed against Frederick's coat. "Martha's...heart?" I croaked the words.

"Will remain safe." He pulled me back far enough to kiss my hair, my temple. His lips gritty against my closed eyelids.

"Livvie?" I coughed as the dust settled around us, in my lungs. Panic rose in my chest. Where was she? Had she made it to Pendle Street?

"She's with my sister." *Livvie was safe.* I sank against him. Then, remembering the man I'd feared would hurt her, I tried to turn towards the corner where Dr. Harrison had crumpled. Shafts of dusty light obstructed my view. "Is he...?"

"He can't hurt us." Frederick pulled me into his lap. His arm blocked the view of the remaining rubble as his hand rubbed circles on my back. Exhaustion tore through my limbs, and my eyelids fluttered closed. So heavy.

Frederick's lips touched my forehead. "How did you do this, Adelaide?"

Unable to keep my eyes open any longer, I drifted towards unconsciousness. Soft, velvety darkness slipped around me as I pushed the words past my cracked lips. "*I'm* the Fairshaw Master."

CHAPTER 43

Frederick

Adelaide's confession tumbled through my mind as I carried her to her old room, tucked her under the quilts, and with one last kiss to her relaxed brow, left her in Elizabeth's care. *How could my wife be the Fairshaw Master? Had she had her powers the whole time we'd been married?*

I brought Nicholas to Liv's old rooms, and sent a servant to fetch Martha. When she arrived her words were far from gentle, but I could easily forgive her. I'd seen the fear in her eyes as she'd looked over Nicholas's injuries, and imagined my own words would have held as much venom if she'd ever let Adelaide sustain similar ones.

But Adelaide's wounds had healed, or so Liv had claimed as she'd ran to meet me at the gates. I'd enlisted Stonier's help to bring Dr. Harrison's body home, but now that I was back, I needed to see my wife for myself. The burning desire to touch her, to assure myself she was as strong and healthy as before, propelled me through the halls to her bedchamber. Finding it empty, I went to the gardens next.

My hand wrapped around cold iron as I pulled the gate open.

Surrounded by flowering herbs and blooming roses, Adelaide looked every bit the part of wealthy heiress. But the Fairshaw Master? My boots kicked up rocks as I stepped down the gravel path. The sweet perfume of flowers of every origin filled the air. The trickling sound of the water fountain joined with the humming of bees—the sunlit summer day a symphony all its own. And she surpassed it all.

I love you.

She turned at the sound of my footsteps, and her eyes widened. But when she said my name, her voice held none of the confidence I wanted for the woman I loved. Finally close enough to touch her, I wrapped my hand around hers. The light stroke of her thumb over my fingers skittered across my skin as if there was magic between us too.

Perhaps the greatest magic of all.

"Adelaide." I spoke her name like an incantation. The highborn, magnificent woman I'd first laid eyes on paled in comparison to the foul-mouthed, passionate one I'd come to know.

I love you.

I'd found her beautiful from the time I'd stood dumbfounded and gawking by her window. By the time I'd pledged to lay down my life for hers, her beauty had already increased tenfold from that first day. But nothing could have prepared me for the woman standing in front of me now, or the emotion clogging my throat as I took her in.

Her hair was sunshine, her eyes twin fires of blue. Her full lips formed words I couldn't hear for looking at her—her beauty was so loud. Laughter like tinkling silver bells found my ears at last, and I gazed into her eyes.

"Are you even listening to me?"

I shook my head, then reached one bandaged hand out to touch her while pulling her closer with the other. My finger trailed the softness of her jaw, and my gut tightened at her small gasp. "You're beautiful." *Was this rough voice mine?*

"You're a dolt." But her soft voice belied her words, as did the tender way her eyes roved over my face.

My hand slid to her shoulder, dragging her up against me, and she stepped into my embrace without hesitation. The scent of her skin blasted my senses, making me want to forget everything but *now* and *her*.

But I needed more questions answered before I lost

myself in this moment. "How did you kill Dr. Harrison?"

Her body stiffened in my arms, but she didn't pull away. I ran my hand over the back of her head, down her spine, moving my fingers in soothing circles. "I'm not assigning blame, love. I just need to understand."

"The Fairshaw magic bends to the will of the Fairshaw Master. I think it just followed my hatred for him when he confessed to killing the cat." Her words were a breath, but they seemed to ring through the garden.

"But if he caught it first, why not just take the key? He'd have all the wealth and prestige he'd want." *And the chance to kill the woman I loved.* My arms tightened around Adelaide as fresh anger pulsed through my body.

"The Fairshaw magic is too pure to yield to the kind of man Dr. Harrison was. All I can think is that he found the cat and it refused him the key."

"So he killed it?" I tried to wrap my head around her words, his actions.

Her eyes filled with tears. "I'm so sorry Frederick. He was everything I accused you of. Ruthless, power-hungry—a murderer."

Her cheeks glistened, and I shook my head, kissed her temple again. "Shh, love. I told you I forgave you."

"But you—" Her words broke off on a sob.

"What, love?"

"You don't know how much I...hated you."

I couldn't help the grin that spread on my face. I pushed a strand of blonde out of her eyes. "Oh, I knew." Her cheeks flushed as she pulled away and slugged my shoulder. I laughed, but the laugh died as I remembered what she'd experienced these past weeks. How close she'd come to dying. "Did you know you could be the Fairshaw? I thought the magic passed down only through male heirs."

She looked down. "I don't think I *could* be the heir until the cat was killed by evil. The Fairshaw magic couldn't transfer to an evil man, so it returned to the Fairshaw bloodline—even a woman."

I stilled. If she was right, then... "I was never the Fairshaw."

Her eyes widened as she shook her head. "I'm sorry, Frederick."

I frowned. "What for?"

She bit her lip. "Your ambition. You wanted to be the Fairshaw Master."

I shook my head. "I wanted to provide for my sisters. Something tells me I'll still be able to do that."

"Of course you will. But you can't tell me you didn't want the power and knowledge of the Fairshaw Master, too?"

"I wanted to be yours more." She tilted her face up, and for a moment, her warm mouth pressed against mine was all I could think about.

We had so much time—so many kisses—to make up for.

My pulse hammered in my ears. I framed her face, bent my head, and—pulled back. "One more question. How did you find out about your powers? I don't understand how you became so sick if you were the Fairshaw all along."

"I was too sick at first. When your sacrifice healed me, I think I'd have felt the magic sooner if not for the medicine he kept giving me."

Anger burned through my chest. "He didn't heal you at all, did he? He was trying to kill you the whole time—and I let him."

Her eyes held a world of sadness. "The Fairshaw magic was the only thing that kept him from killing me with his draughts. I think he was annoyed it was taking so long." She let out a little laugh, but I saw the hurt in her eyes.

"I'm going to kill him!"

Amusement slipped into her expression, warring with the pain written there. "You're too late this time, my love." *And thank God for that.* Not that I wouldn't gladly kill him again. Pushing the thought of murder to the back of my mind, I moved a lock of hair off her face.

"What about the Fairshaw Cat? Did my sacrifice heal it too?"

Her eyes glittered. "I *am* the cat."

"What? So you could have told me where it was the whole time?"

Her laughter rang out, warming the air I pulled into my lungs. "No. I wasn't the cat then. The Fairshaw Cat is only the manifestation of the magic when there is no rightful heir. Now that I am the Fairshaw Master, the magic is in me."

I kissed the top of her head, careful to avoid the blue sparks that trailed her hairline. "You're letting off sparks. Did he ever see that?"

She shrugged, tucking herself closer. "I don't think so. Or maybe he thought they were a sign that I was dying."

I didn't know whether to laugh at Dr. Harrison's stupidity in trying to kill the Fairshaw Master, or cry because my own foolishness had made it easier for him. "I thought you were angry with me. If I had come to you before…"

She shook her head. "It's no matter now. I'm safe, and I'm yours."

I let out a deep breath as her words echoed through my mind. "Thank God."

I tugged her close and kissed her like I'd never kissed her before—like I'd never stop kissing her again. And as my hands tunneled into her hair and roamed over every part of her I'd feared I'd never touch again, I knew I'd have no reason to.

She was safe. And I was finally hers.

CHAPTER 44

Adelaide

3 weeks later

The sweet, musky smell of aged paper and ink filled my nostrils as I turned over another yellowed page. I no longer needed stories to escape from my life, but as the thrill of adventure rolled through my stomach, I let the words carry me—

"Adelaide, you've read that book so many times before." Frederick's warm breath in my ear tugged me back to reality, where I was reading tucked into his side on a bench in the garden.

I sighed. "The same can be said for you kissing me, and you haven't lost interest yet."

"And I won't." He growled and tightened his arm around me as he pressed a kiss to my hair. My ear. My neck. Goosebumps sprang out on my skin, and I shivered. "Frederick, I can't concentrate like this. I told you I'm going to finish this chapter before I kiss you."

"I'd like to challenge that statement, Mrs. Holloway." His voice lowered to a delicious timbre. Then, in one quick move, his strong arms wrapped around me and I was hoisted into the air. I squealed as my book flew out of my hands.

"Frederick! That was a first edition!" I stretched my neck and searched for the volume on the ground. The pollen-drunk buzz of bumble bees filled the air, and the heavy fragrance of roses wafted over the half circle of blooming bushes that framed our favorite spot in the Library gardens. We'd spent plenty of time here in the three weeks that had passed since Frederick had moved back in.

His lips brushed mine. "I'm so sorry, love. Are you sure we don't have another?" His voice turned huskier. "We could go inside and look for it?"

I let out a huff, and tried to keep a smile out of my voice. "That's…not what you'll do if we go inside."

He grinned against my mouth, and shifted his grip on me. "Very astute, my love. Now—"

A throat cleared behind us, and Frederick swung us around. My gaze fell on our butler inspecting the mass of fluffy pink and white peonies by the foot path. My cheeks burned. How much had he overheard?

"Mistress Fairshaw, Mr. Holloway. Am I interrupting?"

His scrutiny moved to the bright snapdragons I was certain matched the high color in my cheeks. We spoke at the same time, Frederick's yes colliding with my no.

"Let me down, Frederick." I hissed the words in his ear. He grinned and pressed another kiss to my cheek, earning himself a smack to his shoulder. The butler maintained his sudden botany interest without batting an eye, as if this scenario was nothing out of the ordinary. *Which was true.* I narrowed my eyes at my husband.

Then, for the sake of the poor man in our employ, I smiled and pretended I had no plans to throttle my husband as soon as we were alone. "What is it, Stonier?"

"Mr. and Mrs. Cromwell have arrived, Mistress Fairshaw. They are presently in the hall. Shall I show them to the gardens?"

"Yes, please. Thank you, Stonier."

"Of course, Mistress Fairshaw." He tipped his balding head in a bow.

As soon as he was out of earshot I turned my scowl on Frederick. "You need to put me down."

He groaned. "Isn't it enough that the bloke married my sister, does he need to interrupt our rare quiet moments, too?"

"We *invited* them, Frederick." I squirmed in his arms. I didn't want to greet any more people from my undignified position, but as approaching footsteps sounded, I sighed in defeat.

The iron gates were barely visible under the flowering vines weaving through them, but as they opened, Martha entered on the arm of her blacksmith husband. Gone were her hunched shoulders and the shadows under her eyes, and in their place was a glow of pure happiness. Frederick's posture relaxed as if he'd noted the same change in her. I pressed my cheek against his shoulder, knowing how much their years in poverty weighed on him.

"Adelaide, are you all right? Why is my brother carrying you?" Martha's voice was full of concern.

I rolled my eyes. "Your brother is a barbarian, is all. He just ruined a first edition of Robinson Crusoe." I nodded to the book, pages splayed, in the bed of red geraniums.

"Frederick James Holloway!" Martha gasped, let go of Nicholas's arm, and bent to pick up the discarded book. She inspected it for signs of damage, brushed a red petal off it, and handed it to me. "I think it might be all right."

Frederick finally lowered me to the ground but didn't let go. I leaned against his solid chest, and his voice rumbled against my back. "We live in the Fairshaw Library. Surely we have another."

Martha and I sighed in unison, and she sent me an apologetic look. "I tried my best, Adelaide."

I groaned, much louder than strictly necessary. "I'm still trying my best, Martha. He's not really improving."

Martha's straight face slipped, and she grinned.

"Very funny." Frederick's voice rumbled against my back, and I turned in time to see the scowl he directed at his sister. He turned to Nicholas. "Don't say I didn't warn you."

Nicholas's gaze softened as his eyes met Martha's, and magic much deeper than any found in the Fairshaw Library sparked in the air between them. "I'm quite happy, Master Holloway."

A girly squeal accompanied the sound of running feet, and in the next moment, a rosy-cheeked Livvie bounded through the gate. She wrapped her arms around Martha's waist and pressed her cheek against her front. "Martha! I've missed you."

Martha bent and folded her arms around the little girl. "I've missed you, too, love." The Pendle Street apartment sat empty now that Livvie lived at the Fairshaw Library and Martha, who already wore her gown quite loosely, had moved in with Nicholas and his father.

Frederick bent his head to whisper in my ear. "Explain to me again about the magic you have as the Fairshaw Master. Can it make us invisible?"

Frowning, I turned in his arms until I faced him. "Why in the world would we need to be invisible?"

He grinned wickedly at me, and my stomach flipped. He tipped my chin up with his finger, and let his dark eyes roam over my face. "So that I can do this." He pressed his lips to mine, blocking out the twitter of birds in the trees, the flower-scented air, and Livvie's exasperated groan.

Magic sparked in my blood, tingled through my veins and tilted the earth on its axis, until the only solid points in the world were his mouth, his hands, his kiss. The man who had climbed my window to own the Fairshaw magic pulled back. I met his gaze, so full of love that tears welled in my eyes.

His hunt for the Fairshaw Cat might not have brought him the magic he'd sought, but it had gifted him magic all the same. Magic that simmered in the space between us, skittered over my skin as his hands framed my face.

And then filled the very air as he spoke.

"I. Love. You."

EPILOGUE

Frederick

Three years later

The window was open. I braced my weight on either side of the open shutters, and my mouth dropped at the sight that met me. Adelaide Fairshaw stood facing away from the window, hair unbound and wearing only a dressing gown.

She leaned forward to touch her fingertips to the surface of the water in the large copper bathtub—as if she couldn't judge its temperature from the rising swirls of heat.

That day three years ago when I'd first climbed up to this windowsill, I hadn't been in the hunt for a bride. But today?

Today, I was.

I shifted more of my weight into the arm resting on the Library windowsill, and tilting my head, watched my wife.

She still drew and bound my attention with invisible strings. Thick, golden ringlets cascaded down her back, and the elaborate dressing gown outlined curves I now knew—though not well enough. Never well enough.

Shaking the water droplets off her fingers, she moved to loosen the tasseled cord around her not-so-slender waist. But my conscience was quiet this time—there was no need for my eyes to drop from the mesmerizing sight. My pulse kicked up a notch as her dressing gown lowered, revealing her shoulders, the small of her back, widening hips—a startled laugh sounded as she yanked the fabric up.

I met her eyes in the mirror behind the tub. She clutched her dressing gown closed and whirled on me, eyes sparking with mischief and her mouth twisted in a smirk that heated my blood. And, Fairshaw Master or not, her curses still singed the air. But this day, her eyes shot no daggers. "Have you no decency, Frederick Fairshaw?"

I smirked. "Very little, I'm afraid."

She glanced toward the cradle at the end of our bed, but the babe she'd birthed me four short months ago made no noise. Yet. Adelaide's lips parted, and she tugged the lower one between her teeth. Then she lunged as if to attack. I shifted away on instinct, but I had too much to live for to let her startle me into falling.

Grinning like a fool, I gazed up at her. "It's been lovely making your acquaintance, Lady Fairshaw, but I'm afraid your tricks don't work on me as they used to." Her eyebrows lifted as if this was a challenge she'd rise to.

My eyes trailed over the features I loved. "What's this? No more cursing out your dock-trash husband?"

A mischievous smile lit her eyes. "I'll leave the cursing to you this time." She pulled the cord, the dressing gown slipped from her shoulders—and I did.

THE END

A Note from the Author

Thank you for reading this little piece of my heart. I truly hope you enjoyed your reading as much as enjoyed the writing!

If you did, please consider leaving a review on Amazon or Goodreads. It helps me so much! Thank you!

ᴀCKNOWLEDGEMENTS

This book was supposed to be my first book, and as such, I dedicated it to the man whose extensive library inspired it, my grandfather, Besten (5/23/1933 - 10/22/2020). I don't know how many books were in that library when he died—books several hundred years old and books brand new. I dreamed for years of mine, one day, being among them. They are not, but the first words of The Fairshaw Library are, as they've been from the beginning:

For Besten, Per Skjaeveland, whose love of words and reading rivals my own.

I know it's in no way unnatural to leave earth at the age of 87, but I wish so badly I had more time with him. I never felt like my words were adequate to tell him how much his support meant to me, the years he and my grandmother supported me were the darkest of my life, and I can say with absolute confidence that I would not have found a way to keep going if not for their help. And, the book you're holding would not be either.

The books Besten let me borrow from his extensive library, the same ones that shaped my writing voice, are on my shelf now. He has been gone almost two years, but our mutual love of books lives on, as does his memory.

And then it's everyone else. Writing may seem like a solitary occupation, but it's really not. And the people I've met along the way have been my favorite part of this journey.

If you are one of the people who helped this book become what it is, I'm beyond thankful to you.

First of all, Thank you, Lord, for every breath in my lungs. There would be no books without you.

Many thanks also to:

My grandmother, Farmor—for your legacy of love, kindness, and persistence. You've given me a lot to live up to, and I'm so thankful for the years we had. It hurts every day that there are no more.

My grandmother, Mormor—for your friendship, your love, for telling me my piercing looks pretty, even though you didn't like the idea of it. I honestly don't know what I will ever do without you.

My grandfather, Morfar—for insisting on reading my books first. I hope you enjoy this one, too!

My son, Kieran—for hyping up me and my book so much. I know you're disappointed we're not millionaires yet, but being able to discuss this book with you while you've been embarking on your own journey of falling in love with books and reading has meant the world to me. I love you so much more than you'll ever know.

Jenni Sauer—this book would never be what it is without you. I can't thank you enough for your help, your love, your wealth of knowledge on stickers and Victorian era novels, your patience in my numerous attacks of imposter syndrome, and for raising my friendship and relationship standards forever.

Tara Knott—for your never-ending support, for always being up for a trip to the ocean (and CVS), for crying as hard as I do over every amazing turn on this author journey. I love you.

Lauren Wyant—for supporting me in every way despite my objectively terrible advice about shoe laces. Thank you for being my daily dose of sanity and for teaching me all your excellent terrorist negotiation tactics.

Amanda Thornell—where do I start? For being my constant commiserater, bringer of hope to my world, and incredible long distance hugger. Your support has been 100% invaluable and beautifical.

Leeah Fisher—Your feedback gave me so much faith in this book. Keep sending me favorite pics, please. I love you always.

My Virtual Roommate, Ingjerd Løvgren Auestad—for keeping alive the notion that long distance relationships are a total piece of cake. And for all the reindeer photos.

Cat Wiant—you will forever be my favorite Cat. There are significantly more flowers in this book, but please don't take it personally. I even included snapdragons (that turn into skulls when they vilt). Your support means the world to me.

My UnWriters not previously mentioned (Jenny Baldwin, Vicky Esquivel, Kayleigh Wilkes, and Desarae Wisnoski)—for being in my corner. I have a shelf ready to fill with our books.

Selina R. Gonzalez—for your magical formatting skills. Thank you for your patience and business knowledge. You have been a joy to work with.

Sara Ella—For your many helpful suggestions on my early drafts.

My editor, Savanna Roberts—for understanding exactly where my story was coming from, and where it needed to go. Your pterodactyl screeches were everything I didn't know I needed. I refuse to publish a book without your input, so please never stop editing.

My Beta Readers not previously mentioned (Stephanie Lynn, Rachel Bishop, and Melynne Vick)—for taking time out of your busy schedules to read the early version of this story, and for your encouraging feedback.

Marie, our imaginary kitchen maid—for always leaving me to clean up the kitchen. Actually, thanks for nothing, Marie.

ABOUT THE AUTHOR

AUSTIN RYAN was born and raised in Norway, but has no previous experience hunting for magical cats in the English countryside. After a childhood of desperately longing to be English, she accidentally wrote a novel about a wealthy heiress, a magical library, and the opportunistic dock-worker the heroine (and the author) falls madly in love with. The Fairshaw Library is her second full-length novel.

Austin lives in Connecticut, surrounded by overflowing bookshelves, Christmas lights, and sparkly things.

When she is not editing words for other authors, getting lost in their stories, or writing her own, you can find her on adventures with her very favorite child, painting things that don't need to be painted, and spending hours down by the ocean.

You can connect with Austin at AuthorAustinRyan.com
Facebook: facebook.com/AuthorAustinRyan
Instagram: instagram.com/authoraustinryan/
Goodreads: goodreads.com/austinryan